I0662820

Courteous, courageous and commanding—
these heroes lay it all on the line for the
people they love in more than fifty stories about
loyalty, bravery and romance.
Don't miss a single one!

MEN
in
UNIFORM

STELLA BAGWELL

THE WHITE NIGHT

Published by Silhouette Books
America's Publisher of Contemporary Romance

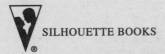

SILHOUETTE BOOKS

Recycling programs for this product may not exist in your area.

ISBN-13: 978-0-373-36271-4

THE WHITE NIGHT

Visit Silhouette Books at www.eHarlequin.com

Printed in U.S.A.

STELLA BAGWELL

has written more than seventy novels for Silhouette Books. She credits her loyal readers and hopes her stories have brightened their lives in some small way.

A cowgirl through and through, she loves to watch old Westerns, and has recently learned how to rope a steer. Her days begin and end helping her husband care for a beloved herd of horses on their little ranch located on the south Texas coast. When she's not ropin' and ridin', you'll find her at her desk, creating her next tale of love.

The couple have a son, who is a high school math teacher and athletic coach.

To my editor, Tara Hughes Gavin,
for her kindness, patience and wonderful insight.
And most of all, for allowing me to
write with all my heart.

Chapter One

Eve Crawford pulled back on the throttle until the red fishing boat was merely idling, drifting with the current of the lake. Fog, thick, white and eerie, swirled around her and the sixteen-foot craft.

Muttering a curse under her breath, she stood, keeping a tentative hand on the wheel. She could see no more than four, maybe five, feet in any direction. It would be impossible to cross three miles of lake in this pea soup without becoming lost or risking an accident.

She'd been foolish to start back home at this late hour in the evening, especially with a thunderstorm just breaking. But when she'd left her friend Julie's house in Zwolle, the rain had stopped completely and Eve had decided the storm was over.

Maybe the storm had ended, but the foggy clouds

had decided to hang around and make Toledo Bend Reservoir their home for at least a few more hours.

It was a good thing her father, Burl, was out of town. He'd have been worried if she hadn't arrived home on time. As it was, no one even knew she was on the lake except Julie, and she had left to drive to Natchitoches, so that counted her out, also.

So no one would know she was stranded. But there was hardly anything Eve could do about that now. In fact, she was at a loss to know *what* to do. Eve had been in fog before, but not fog of this density. It was as if she'd been blindfolded, spun around, then left to grope her way back to land.

Cutting the motor, Eve stood stock-still and listened for sounds—any sounds that might hint at where she was. For about a half mile she'd been traveling in a southwesterly direction. Since the fog had forced her to stop, however, she'd been drifting. How far, or in what direction, she wasn't sure.

One thing Eve was certain of was that somehow she had to keep going. The lake was filled with rotten trees, fallen logs and hidden tree trunks that were just beneath the water's surface. Any one of them could rip a boat open in a matter of seconds. Her first priority was to find land, any land, and moor the boat. She could always walk home, if need be.

For the next thirty minutes Eve battled the fog and the shrouded trees that jutted out of the water like menacing ghosts lying in waiting for her to make a wrong turn.

Her arms ached from working the steering wheel and the gas throttle. Night was falling quickly, making visibility even worse. She longed to burst into frustrated tears, but that would only make matters worse.

She had to keep her senses about her if she planned to come out of this safe and sound.

The next instant the boat lurched, and Eve was slammed against the steering wheel. It took a few moments for her to figure out she'd crashed into something.

Gulping in a shaky breath, Eve cut the motor and walked out onto the nose of the boat. Two tree trunks had caused the rude interruption. But luckily, from the look of things, nothing was severely damaged—except, perhaps, her equilibrium.

Straightening to her full height, she pushed her damp hair away from her face and peered into the white obscurity. She could see nothing.

"Damn! Damn!"

Her frustrated words were suddenly answered by the bark of a dog. One that was obviously very close by. She was near land! Thank God!

"Hello! Is anyone there?" she yelled.

The only answer was the dog's low baying. Eve welcomed the sound and used it to steer her way to the bank.

She'd never been so relieved when she was finally able to jump over the nose of the boat and wade onto the solid shore.

The dog, a black and tan hound, was beside her by the time she'd hauled in the boat and tied the mooring rope around the snag of a dead tree.

"Hello, pretty thing," she said to the dog. "I think you just saved my life."

The dog whined and wagged his tail in a friendly manner. Eve reached out to pat his head just as a voice sounded behind her.

"I doubt Rebel realizes it."

Startled, Eve spun around in search of the voice. It came eerily out of the fog, followed by the crunching and snapping of leaves and twigs.

A figure, tall and masculine, suddenly materialized in the mist. Eve blinked and involuntarily stepped back.

"What are you doing out here?" he asked when she failed to say anything.

"Going home. I got lost in the fog," she replied a little warily.

His dark eyes took slow appraisal of her damp brown hair, flushed cheeks and round, gray eyes. He figured she was in her early twenties, but it would have been difficult to pinpoint her exact age.

"It was a foolhardy thing to start home in this. Didn't anyone warn you about fog on this lake?"

He was Texan. That much she could hear in his voice. But he was not from east Texas; he didn't drawl his *r*'s enough. So how did he know about this lake? She'd lived here all her life, and she didn't ever remember seeing this man before.

"Yes, I know about the fog. But when I left Zwolle there wasn't any fog. It crept in on me before I knew it."

He knew how easily that could happen. "Where were you headed?"

"Pine Ridge Marina," she said while glancing around her. Nothing looked familiar, not the land, or the man.

"You're way off track, lady. You're still in Louisiana. I'd say you're at least five or more miles from Pine Ridge."

"Five miles!" Eve groaned and thrust her tangled hair away from her face. "It looks like I have a long wait ahead of me."

She turned and climbed back into the boat. He watched as she flipped down one of the seats and began to search through the odds and ends stored in the compartment underneath.

She was tall and slender, almost delicate in appearance, but something told him that the aura of soft femininity was deceptive. She was wearing a pair of white jeans that were wet from the knees down from when she'd jumped out and tugged the boat onto the shore. Above the jeans was a navy blue blouse with the sleeves pushed up over her elbows.

Eve pulled out an olive-green slicker and tossed it over her arm. She looked back at the stranger.

"Are there any houses nearby?"

He shook his head. "None that I know of."

"How did you get here?"

"Horse."

She raised her brows but made no comment. For the first time Eve let herself look at him.

He was in his early thirties, she decided. His complexion was very dark, and his hair, which was combed back from his face, was straight and black. Not raven colored, but a soft, warm black. As his hair covered the back of his neck, it was too long to be tidy. But it was very shiny, indicating a healthy vitality that could also be seen in his thick shoulders and arms, his trim waist and long, muscular thighs.

"I have a camp about a hundred yards from here," he said. "You're welcome to come over and wait out the fog."

Eve's eyes were riveted to the stranger's face. He had an arresting set of features. He wasn't handsome, but there was a compelling masculinity about him. Jet-black brows grew thick and straight over a pair of hazel eyes. A large, rather hawkish nose led to a pair of well-carved lips. The lower one was just full enough to curve with a subtle hint of sensuality. The top lip was thinner, although a jagged scar on the right side gave it a fuller impression.

She shivered ever so slightly while thinking she'd never before encountered such a face, or one that fascinated her so completely.

"It's all right," he said. "I'm harmless. Rebel will vouch for me."

Eve realized she still hadn't spoken and that he thought she was frightened. Eve had never been frightened of anyone.

"I didn't think you were," she said politely, then jumped off the nose of the boat to land about six inches from the water's edge. "And I'd be grateful to share your camp."

"This way," he said to her, then turned and headed into the dense woods.

It was dark now. Eve followed him closely, matching her steps to his in case a water moccasin should be lying near. The dog, Rebel, followed Eve, sniffing at her jeans as if to assure himself that she was acceptable and safe to let around his master.

In less than three minutes they walked into a small clearing. A burgundy-colored dome tent was set up there, with a small camp fire nearby.

The man opened a folding camp chair and placed it near the fire for Eve. She thanked him and sat down.

While she settled herself, he dragged up a galvanized bucket, turned it upside down and promptly used it for his seat. The hound flopped down at his feet.

"My name is Eve," she told him. "Eve Crawford."

Eve. The name suited her, he thought. She had a quiet, subtle beauty. One that didn't shout, but instead grew on a person.

"People call me Elliot," he said.

She nodded and looked away from him. Her face was flushed, but she knew the fire masked the color on her cheeks.

"Are you new around here?" she asked. There were lots of people who migrated to the lake area in the winter. Since Toledo Bend was located on the Texas-Lousiana border, it was far enough south to miss most of the cold weather. Yet it was April now, and Eve instinctively knew that this stranger was not a snowbird.

"In a way. I used to live around here."

He didn't offer more, and Eve refrained from asking. She had the feeling he was a reticent person, and reticent people didn't like pryers.

"My dad and I have run the Pine Ridge Marina," she told him, "for about ten years."

His brown-green eyes settled on her face. She noticed his lashed were thick, the color of soot. The black veil hid the sharp gleam with which he studied her.

"You were out fishing?" he asked.

Eve shook her head. "I'd been over to Zwolle to see a friend. It saves at least ten miles to go across the lake instead of driving around on the highway," she explained. "I've never been in fog this thick. No matter how well you know the lake, it doesn't do you any good if you can't see where you're going."

"No, I suppose not."

She shifted on the seat and glanced down at the fire. It smelled like hickory smoke, and she wondered if he'd already eaten supper. Her eyes slipped back to his face.

"Er, what are you doing out here? Getting in some weekend fishing?"

His lips pursed with faint amusement. "No. I'm not a fisherman."

The answer did not surprise Eve. He looked nothing like a fisherman. He was wearing a black T-shirt with the words Harley-Davidson written across the front. It was tucked into a pair of faded jeans that sported a small, three-cornered tear on one thigh. His feet were covered with a pair of black cowboy boots, the heels and soles caked with bayou mud.

"Oh." It was the only thing she could think to say.

His mouth twisted wryly. "I'm babysitting alligators," he said.

She gave him a straightforward stare. "Gators? Are you poaching?"

The slant of his grin was dry and mocking. "Not hardly. I'm here to see if they are being poached."

"You don't look like you work for the Game and Fish Commission."

His grin deepened, as though he enjoyed having Eve appraise him. She wondered about that.

"I don't," he said. "But an old friend does. I'm doing it as a favor for him."

Eve looked at him with new eyes. So he didn't kill or maim. He was a stranger to this area even though he'd once lived here, he'd said. And he knew someone in the Game and Fish Commission. Not much to know about a man with whom you were sharing a campfire, miles from nowhere.

She pushed back the wave of brown hair that had fallen in her face and gave him a sidelong glance. The fire-glow did nothing to soften the toughness of his face, yet Eve found herself trusting him—and liking him.

"Do you think the fog will lift?"

His eyes met hers. "Maybe. But it won't do you much good. It's going to start raining again."

Her brows lifted. "How do you know that?"

He shrugged and smiled with a bit of arrogance. "I just do. Rebel told me."

Eve glanced at the black and tan animal. The dog was sound asleep, his nose nudged up against the stranger's boot heels.

"Do you have a family, Elliot?" she asked.

For a moment his eyes pierced hers. Then suddenly he leaned forward and pulled a wire rack across the crackling flames.

Eve watched as he reached for a blue graniteware coffee pot set to one side of the fire. Deftly he put it on the rack to heat. His hands were large, and the backs were sprinkled with black hair, as were his arms. There were no rings on his fingers, although that did not necessarily mean anything.

"I have myself," he told her after a few moments.

Eve was certain she'd never heard anything so sad or disturbing.

Elliot looked up to find her staring at him, and in that moment he was more aware of what he'd become than he'd ever been before. He was alone. Alone in more ways than this soft woman could ever imagine.

"Are you hungry, Miss Eve?"

"Well, er, do you have anything handy?"

With a shake of his head, he said, "I was about to cook when Rebel found you."

She put the slicker, which had been lying across her

lap, to one side of her chair and rose to her feet. "Then let me," she suggested. "I'm a good cook."

His brows lifted, and, fascinated, she watched as his lips curved into the semblance of a smile. She wondered how he'd gotten the scar. However it had happened, the injury hadn't affected his teeth. They were very white and even, and good to look at. Just like the rest of him. She took a deep breath and let it out slowly.

"Is that brag or fact?"

She smiled fully at him, the movement lighting up her eyes and face. Elliot decided her gray eyes were beautiful. They seemed to see everything. How much of him could she see?

"Fact," she answered. "I've been cooking since I was ten."

With sudden decision, he got to this feet. "Here's an ice chest. Pick out what you want."

She followed him to the side of the tent. "You didn't bring this here on horseback," she said, kneeling down to search through the ice chest.

"I bring supplies in with a Jeep," he told her.

"You leave your camp set up here all the time?" she asked as she began to sift through the food items.

"I move occasionally."

Eve digested his words as she chose a package wrapped in white paper. She didn't have to open it to know it contained smoked slab bacon.

While she gathered other items to go with the meat, Elliot put out a couple of skillets. In a matter of minutes she was frying potatoes and onions in one skillet, bacon in the other.

"Did you cook out of necessity or pleasure?" he

asked as he sat back on the bucket and crossed his boots lazily out in front of him.

"Both," she answered. She felt his eyes watching her as she worked, but Eve didn't mind.

She felt very safe with him, even though he was a stranger and they were secluded in the woods.

"My mother died when I was very young. I don't even remember her. Daddy taught me to cook. I'd drag up a chair and stand beside him at the cabinet."

"You have brothers or sisters?"

For some reason this man thought it was okay to question her, which was strange, she thought, because it was obvious to her that he didn't want any questions tossed at him.

"One brother," she told him. "He's older. This past year he married and moved away. I miss him."

Yes, she would, he thought. He could tell she loved people. Her family probably meant a great deal to her. He realized it had been a long time since he'd been around someone like her—a woman like her.

"You cook over that camp fire like you've done it before," he said, watching her stir the potatoes. Her wrists and hands were fine-boned, her skin a light rosy beige. She had a gentle grace about her. His mouth twisted wryly as he noticed Rebel had opened his bloodshot eyes to watch her, too.

"Of course I've done it before. My brother and I used to camp quite a bit."

"I guess that's over with, since he's gone now?"

She looked over at him and smiled. "I thought so. But here I am doing it again."

He smiled faintly at that, and Eve watched thick lashes fall against his eyes.

The smells of frying bacon and potatoes and coffee permeated the fog-shrouded woods around them. Frogs sang in glorious worship to the rain as the fire hissed and crackled with gentle warmth.

Elliot brought out dishes while Eve heated a can of pork and beans in the skillet in which she'd fried the bacon. In no time they were balancing full plates on their knees.

"How far had you been traveling on the lake when you heard Rebel?" he asked.

"Forty minutes at least," she said. "I must have gotten turned around right at the start."

He nodded and bit into a piece of bacon. Eve chewed her food and studied him through the corners of her eyes. His arms were terribly strong-looking, the muscles thick and hard. He had the look of a street fighter, and she longed to ask him questions.

"You're from west Texas, aren't you?"

He glanced at her, then back to his plate. "Sorta. Fort Worth. But I was born around here."

A city guy here in the woods, she inwardly mused. What was he doing here? Surely he didn't hunt poachers for a living. Not if he was from Fort Worth.

"How could you tell?" he asked.

The coffee was thick and gritty. Elliot had heated it at least three or four times already that day. He watched her swallow it without a hint of a grimace, and he knew his first judgment of this young woman had been right.

"The *r*'s," she said.

One corner of his lips lifted in wry observation. "Don't they sound Cajun enough for you?"

She shook her head. "I'd say it's been a long time since you've been in this part of Texas."

"Hmm. Well, you could be right."

Even though Eve wanted him to elaborate, she didn't ask him to.

"The wind has started to pick up," Eve said, looking up at the branches moving above their heads. "Maybe the fog will be blown away soon."

"Maybe. But the wind is bringing more rain."

She looked at him with sheer frustration evident in her expression. "That's not what I need to hear. I'll never get home at this rate. Maybe I should just start walking. I can always come back for my boat tomorrow."

He gave her a long look. "Do you know where you are? Do you know most of the land around here is swamp and marshes? And have you counted how many snakes you'd probably stumble over from here to the highway?"

Eve grimaced. "Yes, I know," she conceded with a sigh. "But I feel very helpless just sitting here."

"Does anyone know you were out on the lake?"

"A girlfriend. But she left to go out of town."

He folded his arms across his chest and pushed a piece of wood farther into the fire with the toe of his boot. "You shouldn't have told me that, Miss Eve."

She glanced at him, her eyes wide. "Why? It's the truth. I don't lic to people."

"I might be a man who can't be trusted. How do you know I'm really harmless? How do you know that in the next few minutes I won't turn on you?" Suddenly he leaned closer, and one dark, massive hand threaded its fingers around her throat.

He didn't apply any pressure to hurt her. Instead, his fingers merely pressed into her soft skin. It was a strange sensation to Eve, oddly pleasant, but painfully disconcerting.

"One hard twist and I could snap your pretty neck," he said, his voice low and gravelly.

"I know you wouldn't hurt me," Eve whispered. The skin on his fingers was tough and smelled faintly of bacon and wood smoke.

"No?" he persisted.

There was a strange glitter in his eyes, as if he were daring Eve to say more, as if he wanted to give her the impression that he was not the gentleman she thought he was.

Elliot could feel her pulse thumping beneath his fingers and suddenly felt ashamed of himself. He'd only wanted to make a point, not scare her.

Easing the tension of his fingers, he gently rubbed the skin he'd just pressed. The sensation was soothing and stimulating.

"You haven't answered," he gently reminded her.

She swallowed. "Because I'm a good judge of character, and I know that you're an honest man."

A cynical smile curved his lips. Eve held his gaze as he allowed his fingers to slide down her throat and, finally, away from her.

"Maybe I'll let you go on thinking that," he said cockily.

She smiled and shook her head. "You can't scare me. So there's no use trying to make me believe otherwise."

He suddenly chuckled, surprising Eve with the low sound of pleasure.

"You *were* scared, Miss Eve."

Eve's smile deepened. She decided it would be much safer to let him think her heart was beating out of fear instead of attraction.

The hound abruptly got to its feet and whined. Eve watched the animal sniff the air, then trot off into the woods.

"What's the matter with him?" she asked.

Before Elliot could answer, raindrops began to splatter the already-soggy ground around them.

"Like I told you, Rebel knew it was going to rain," Elliot said.

Eve shot him a bemused look and reached for her raincoat. "I'd better get back to the boat."

"Why?"

She rose to her feet and began to pull on the green slicker. "Because it's starting to rain. I have a tarp in the boat. I'll get under it."

The rain was already growing heavier. Eve saw the drops cling to Elliot's tanned skin and splotch his T-shirt.

"It's dark," he said. "I'd have to walk you back through the woods with the flashlight, and I don't want to do that."

She shrugged and said unaffectedly, "Well, I did say you were honest, but I said nothing about chivalrous."

That produced an outright laugh that had Eve marveling over him. Finally he put his hand on her forearm and said, "We'll get into the tent. After all, I'm honest."

Elliot folded back the flap to the entrance. Eve ducked down and scrambled into the shelter of the tent. He quickly followed.

There was a bedroll in the middle of the floor. Eve sat on one end of the tangled covers, and Elliot squatted on his boot heels and looked out the small opening they'd just passed through.

The rain was falling heavily. Eve listened to it drum against the tent with uncharacteristic helplessness.

"Does this tent leak?" she asked, looking up at the seams.

"I have a rain fly stretched over the top. Although who's to say the rain won't run into the bottom if it gets heavier."

Eve nodded, informing him that she knew what he was talking about. She'd slept on a soggy bedroll more than once on camping trips.

"You picked a bad night to watch for poachers," she told him.

He sat back cross-legged and rested his arms across his knees. "Yeah. It appears that way. But there was nothing to do at the house."

Eve noticed he called it a house instead of home. "Where do you live?"

"On the old Marshall place. Do you know it?"

Eve knew it. The old house was off the beaten track, probably at least ten miles from the marina. The last time she'd been by it, the place had stood empty. But that had been months ago.

"Yes, I remember the Marshalls. Both of them passed on several years back," she recalled.

He looked at her. "They were my grandparents."

Eve blinked as she met his gaze. "You must miss them terribly," she said, then smiled with fond remembrance. "Mrs. Marshall invited me to come out and pick blackberries one spring. I gave her a half gallon of what I'd picked, then two days later she showed up at the marina with a baked cobbler. Your grandparents were very likable people."

"Yeah. Fine people," he repeated lowly.

Eve caught the hint of sadness in his voice and wondered why it should touch her so deeply. She didn't know this man, yet somehow she felt the ache of loneliness he was experiencing at the mention of his grandparents.

"Tell me, Miss Eve, what do you do around here?" he asked.

Her brows drew together as she shifted to remove the slicker. It was hot and muggy inside the tent. Eve was already sweating.

"I help my father run the marina."

"What about socially? I'll bet you have a boyfriend and you're planning on getting married and having a passel of kids."

Eve shook her head. "No. Nothing like that. There's not anyone around here who interests me in that way. Besides, I want to go to college," she confessed.

One of his hands reached up and slicked back the dark hair that threatened to fall in his eyes. "Then why haven't you gone before?"

"Because when I graduated from high school, my brother was in college. Daddy couldn't manage to put two of us through. But now I think I can do it with the help of a grant."

He smiled faintly and leaned back on one elbow. The position made his biceps bulge. Eve let her eyes slide over his arms, then across his chest. The letters of the motorcycle insignia rested on solid muscle. Eve had been around well put together men before, but never one as arresting or intriguing as this one, and she wondered why he should be so different.

"So you want to get smartened up," he said. "And what do you want to do once you get filled with all that knowledge?"

Eve felt herself blushing once again. He made her sound so young and feel even younger. "I want to be a lawyer," she replied with a small measure of pride. "And not one of those ambulance-chasing ones, either.

I want to be a prosecutor. I want to see justice done for all the forgotten victims."

The only light in the tent was the firelight glowing through the tent door, and even that was growing dim as the rain threatened to smother the last of the flames.

Eve watched the faint orange glow play across his features and wondered why she suddenly had the feeling that she'd said something wrong.

"So," he said after a dreadful period of silence. "You want to get into the legal system. You can't know what you're asking for, Miss Eve."

"Of course I do! I know there are still very few women lawyers, but enough to be taken seriously, and—"

"I'm not doubting your ability to become a lawyer," he quickly interrupted. "I'm just saying you wouldn't be happy as one."

Eve couldn't help but smile at him. He seemed so certain about what he was saying. "You couldn't possibly know that, Elliot. You've only just met me."

He rubbed his fingers thoughtfully against his jaw. There was a couple days' growth of beard there, and Eve could hear the raspy sound of it snap beneath his fingers.

"But I do have an idea how you feel. I once knew someone who was the same way. He thought he could make a difference, too. Turned out nobody gave a damn."

Eve wrinkled her nose at him. "That's terribly cynical."

"Yeah. Well, facts are that way sometimes."

Before Eve could respond, he'd raised back up from the elbow to look outside. "It looks like the rain has set in for the night."

Eve was so alarmed by his words that she scooted forward and nearly banged her head against his in order to see for herself.

It was indeed still pouring. Eve groaned in despair as she watched the drops dancing across the puddles forming outside the tent.

"What am I going to do, Elliot? There's no way I can get home in this."

It had been a long time since Elliot had been this close to a woman. The faint scent of roses drifted from her skin and hair. Surprisingly, he felt his senses stir, and he quickly told himself that she was not the type of woman he was used to being around. She was not the type of woman for a man like him.

"Well, Miss Eve, I guess you'll just have to sleep with me tonight."

Chapter Two

Like the sweep of a tidal wave, heat rushed from Eve's face all the way to her toes. For the life of her she could not find the strength to break the lock of their gazes. Air rushed from her lungs, leaving them burning and begging her to take another breath.

"Sleep with you," she echoed in a hoarse whisper. "I can't. I've got to get home."

His mouth curled with outright amusement at her innocent response. "How do you propose to do that? Walk five miles through this downpour? Or go back out on the lake in the dark and the fog and the rain? I doubt the bottom of that fiberglass boat would last past the first couple of stumps."

He was right, of course. But that didn't make the situation more acceptable. "I'd be imposing," she said hastily. "I'll go back to the boat and sleep under the tarp."

Elliot could hear a hint of panic in her voice. The urge to protect and reassure her surged up in him. Two qualities he'd thought he had lost were suddenly awakened inside him by a woman named Eve.

"I know you're right, but—"

His smile deepened, which in turn created a set of dimples in his dark cheeks. "You just told me that I wouldn't hurt you."

She sighed. "I know that."

"Don't you believe me?"

"Yes."

"Good. Then it's settled. The safest place for you is here with me."

How strange those words seemed coming from him. She'd had different boyfriends before, but none had ever talked about protecting her or keeping her safe. Was it the circumstances, or the type of man Elliot was that made him want to keep her safe?

Trying to look at the light side, Eve smiled and settled back on her side of the bedroll. "You're being very generous about this—my eating your food and now taking up part of your tent."

Elliot was sorry she'd moved away from him. He was finding her proximity a pleasant distraction. But it was probably for the best, he silently reasoned. If she'd stayed so close for much longer, he would have kissed her. And then she'd have been afraid of him, and he'd have had hell keeping her here.

No, he was going to have to forget about how soft and pretty and charmingly innocent she was. Even more, once she left here, he was going to forget about Eve Crawford entirely.

"I'm not always a gentleman," he drawled. "But I can be when I put my mind to it."

Eve wasn't afraid of him, yet he did disturb her in a way that was both pleasant and uncomfortable. She put it down to the fact that he was so vitally male and she was forced to be close to him.

There was still a faint smile playing around his lips. Her eyes were drawn to the scar. It had been a jagged cut, but the healed welt was not unsightly. Actually, it gave him a rakish look that matched his character.

She smiled at him and said, "I like to think all Texas men are gentlemen."

Elliot's grin turned mocking. "I'd like to think so too, Miss Eve. But that's just not the case at all."

Eve's hair was still damp. She thrust it off her face with her fingers, longing for something to tie it back with. "How long have you been here in east Texas?"

He shrugged. "Six or seven months."

"Do you like it?"

"It's a place just like any other."

She frowned at him. "There's no place like the piney woods of east Texas," she said with slight indignation.

"Sorry," he said. "I guess what I mean is I'm the same in any place."

"That's hard to believe," she countered. "Fort Worth couldn't be anything like Toledo Bend."

He moved away from the tent opening and stretched out on his side some few inches away from Eve.

"It's really the people that make a place," he said.

Eve thought about that for a few moments and had to admit that what he said was more than partially true.

"Why haven't you come over to the marina?" she asked, her eyes on him.

"Because I never had a reason to."

She drew up her legs and linked her fingers around her knees. "Even if you don't fish, we have a good restaurant. You should come eat some time."

His eyelids dropped once again. "I usually cook for myself."

"But eating alone is horrible. Nothing tastes good when you eat alone."

His eyes lifted back to her face. Dry humor quirked his lips. "What will you do when you go to college and become a lawyer? If you don't have a husband, who will eat with you?"

Knowing he was teasing her, she chuckled. "I'll just have to make plenty of friends and make sure they're always around me."

"You like people, don't you." It was more of a statement than a question.

Amazed, Eve stared at him. "Of course I like people. Don't you?"

"Some of them."

She realized his face had become smooth, expressionless, his eyes dark. Eve studied him for long moments. "You can't make me believe you're that tough. If that's what you're trying to do."

"I am tough, Miss Eve."

"Tough to get to know? Tough to get along with? Tough to wake up in the morning?" she asked with a teasing lilt. "If the latter's true, I'll make some coffee in the morning that *will* wake you up."

Eve was relieved to see the serious look on his face change into an amused smile.

"I wish we'd brought the coffeepot in here with us," she went on. "I didn't really get to finish my cup."

"It was old and strong, anyway," he said. "I made it early this morning."

Eve scooted back as far as possible so that she could stretch her legs out in front of her. The bottom part of her jeans was finally beginning to dry. She ran her hands down her shinbones then looked over at him.

"You stayed here last night?" she asked.

"Yes."

"Don't you get lonely?"

"I have Rebel to talk to."

"Rebel talks?"

A dimple appeared at the corner of his mouth. "In dog language."

Eve rested her cheek against her drawn-up knees. "What did you do in Fort Worth?" she ventured onward.

His eyebrows lifted in a sardonic fashion. "Ate, slept, worked."

Eve wrinkled her nose at him. "Are you this way with everyone?"

"Not everyone. I'm telling you more than most."

Eve felt suddenly warm inside. "So. What did you do?"

His hand reached to the left side of his chest as if searching for a pack of cigarettes. There was neither a pocket nor cigarettes there. He dropped his hand and said, "I worked within the municipality."

Eve wanted to ask him more, but she instinctively knew that was all he wanted to tell her. She said, "You used to smoke. Am I making you long for a kick of nicotine?"

Elliot realized she made him long for a number of things, the least of all being a cigarette. "I quit over a year ago, but sometimes I still get the urge for one."

"I'm sorry I've been running on so. I'll be quiet and

listen to the rain, and maybe you'll forget about the cigarette."

Eve closed her eyes, and Elliot rolled to his back and folded his hands against his midsection. He told himself not to think of her, but her presence was filling this tent, his mind, his senses. It was amazing how powerful a woman's presence could be. Powerful and dangerous.

Reluctantly he allowed his eyes to slide back to her. Thick black lashes rested against her cheeks. Her skin was fine-textured, like her hair, which fell in a thick curtain about her face.

He used to think he liked blondes, but Eve's hair was rich and sultry-looking. It would feel soft and real against his fingers. And nice, he figured.

The thought of touching it sent his mind tumbling back to another time and another woman whose blond hair didn't look quite as soft as Eve's, not as casual, not as alluring.

A cold and hollow feeling shot through him as he thought of Renea. When the going had gotten rough, she'd shown her true colors. In his more logical moments, he knew that Renea did not represent most women. But her desertion had hurt him—and the desertion of his friends had scarred him even more.

Elliot slowly rubbed his hand over his face and looked back at Eve. She was still sitting quietly with her eyes closed. No, he decided, Eve would be nothing like Renea.

"Elliot?" Suddenly she lifted her head. "I think it's letting up. Do you think so?"

He realized he'd been so deep in thought that he'd failed to notice the rain slacking off. Rising to his haunches, he looked out the small doorway. "I believe you're right."

Eve's face brightened. "Hallelujah! I can go home."

"You're not going anywhere," he said sternly.

"But if it quits—"

"It's going to start back up. Rebel told me that, too. And then you'd be out in the middle of the lake. Besides, the fog will stay till morning."

In one lithe movement he went out of the opening.

"What are you doing?" she called out of the parting in the tent.

"Making you a cup of coffee. I thought it would be the gentlemanly thing to do," he added.

Quickly she scooted through the tent flap and joined him outside. The rain was only a faint drizzle now, but the dripping leaves made it seem like more. She felt it splatter against her hair and shoulders.

"That isn't necessary, Elliot. I don't have to have coffee. Besides," she pointed out, "the fire is dead."

"I know the fire is dead. That's why I'm building another," he said.

There was a mound covered by a blue plastic tarp some few feet away from the tent. Eve watched him peel back the heavy covering and saw that it protected a stack of firewood.

He loaded a few pieces in his arms and strode back to the circle of rocks.

"If you're going to build the fire, I'll get the coffee ready," she said. "Where's the water and coffee?"

He motioned toward the back of the tent. "There's a three-gallon jug. The coffee's in the chest without the ice."

Eve found it easily and set about cleaning the graniteware pot and refilling it with water and ground coffee.

She noticed as she did that Elliot had been right about the fog. It was still thick, and more than likely would stay that way until morning.

A good dousing of kerosene by Elliot brought the fire to a roar. Once it settled down to burn on its own, he positioned the grate back in place.

Eve set the pot over the hottest part of the fire, then looked up and smiled at Elliot. "You certainly are going to a lot of trouble to make me a cup of coffee."

"You might label me as an inhospitable Texan if I didn't," he said dryly.

Her lips tilted to a deeper smile. "Would that bother you?"

It had been a long time since Elliot had given a damn about what people thought. But for some reason he didn't want Eve to know that. She'd be disillusioned if she really knew him. Why that should bother him, though, he couldn't quite figure out.

"Texas has its image. I wouldn't want to let it down," he answered.

Kneeling down, he removed the lid of the coffeepot and placed a twig of hickory across the opening.

"What's that for?"

"To keep it from boiling over," he said.

"I thought you might be practicing some kind of spiritual ritual or something."

He chuckled. "Just watch the pot, Miss Eve. It won't boil over, I promise."

The chair she had been using before the rain was now sopping wet. Eve fetched her slicker from the tent and draped it over the seat before she sat down. Elliot dried off the bucket with an old rag and pulled it up by the fire.

The evening air was cooler, and the heat from the fire felt good. Eve watched the coffeepot with expectant eyes. Elliot took out a pocketknife from his jeans and began to whittle on a piece of wood.

"Is your hound all right? Where did he go?"

"Hounds know how to shelter themselves. He's buried up in some hollow cypress log right about now."

"Did you have him in Fort Worth?"

He lifted his eyes to look at her. "Do I look like a cruel person?"

"No."

"Well, I would be by keeping a hound in the city," he said. "Rebel would shrivel up and die if he weren't free to roam the woods."

"Are you like Rebel?" she asked.

One corner of his mouth curled up. His eyes glinted back at her. "I believe you would make a good prosecutor," he said.

Eve blushed. "You just look like a man who likes his freedom," she explained.

His eyes drifted away from her and down to the fire. "A man needs to live for himself sometimes. I came back to east Texas to do that."

Eve digested this for long moments. She had the feeling he'd left something behind in Fort Worth. A woman? She wasn't sure, but she definitely wanted to know.

"Do you have a Harley?" she asked, gesturing toward the words on his chest.

He nodded and looked back at her. "It's stored back at my place in Fort Worth," he said.

So he still had a place there. That spoke of ties and connections. Why would he leave that behind for six or seven months?

"I used to have a boyfriend who had a motorcycle. But it was a foreign one. He wasn't well off enough to own a Harley."

Elliot's mouth twisted wryly. "I'm not rich, either, Miss Eve. I just happened to get a good deal on one."

The coffee began to boil, and the rich aroma rose up with the heat of the fire. Eve watched the bubbles roll near the top, but, true to Elliot's prediction, they never passed over the sides. After just a few moments, he set the pot to one side and tossed away the twig.

Eve fetched their rain-filled cups. While she poured out the water and dried them, Elliot put away his pocketknife and chunk of wood.

"Where did you learn about camping?"

"My grandfather Marshall. He used to trap in these woods. I'd tag along and make a pest of myself. I learned a lot from him. And not just about trapping."

"What about your father?"

"Never knew him," he quipped as he took the cup she offered him. "He left my mother and me when I was just a baby."

"Did your mother know why he left?"

"Sure she did. He didn't care about us. He didn't want to be saddled with responsibilities."

Eve carefully sipped the hot coffee and peered at him over the rim of her cup. Talking of his father didn't seem to affect him; it was as though he'd long ago accepted the fact of the man's desertion.

"Is your mother still living?"

He nodded. "In California. Down by San Diego. I don't have too many opportunities to see her. She married again. We talk on the telephone and write sometimes. She's happy, and that's good enough for me."

Eve sighed. "I wish my mother were still alive. I look at her pictures and wonder what kind of personality she had. Daddy said she was like me. I don't know."

Elliot speared his fingers through his hair and raked it back from his face. "What's your dad like?"

Eve smiled with obvious fondness. "He's a big man with a barrel chest and red hair. Most of the time he's pretty easygoing, unless someone riles him."

He smiled faintly at that, and for a few moments they were silent, each digesting what the other had said. After a while, Elliot said, "You make good coffee."

"You make a good fire," she replied.

He smiled again, and Eve got the impression that in spite of his being a loner, he didn't object to her company.

"How old are you, Miss Eve?"

"Twenty-five."

"Hmm. What an old lady you are," he teased.

"How old are you, Elliot?"

He gave her a wry look. "Thirty-one."

"Do you go around asking many women their age?"

"I don't go around asking women anything."

She didn't know what to make of that, so she added, "Actually you're the first man I ever asked that question."

His lips curled with amusement. "So why'd you choose to pick on me?"

"Because I couldn't tell by looking," she answered honestly.

He rubbed his chin, and Eve watched a lock of hair fall over his right eyebrow.

The sudden urge to lean over and kiss him was frighteningly strong.

"You'd better finish your coffee," he suggested. "It's going to start raining again."

She didn't waste time asking him how he knew. Instead, she put her cup aside and reached for the flashlight.

"I have to visit the woods," she explained.

He nodded, not needing to ask why.

It was raining by the time Eve returned. This time Elliot grabbed the coffeepot and their two cups before he followed Eve into the tent.

They took their time drinking the remaining coffee, while rain drummed once again against the tent. Soon the fire was doused. She and Elliot sat in pitch-black darkness.

He turned on the flashlight, reached for a blanket and said, "Well, I guess we'd better try to get some sleep, and maybe the rain will be over by morning."

Eve nodded, feeling suddenly awkward. "You take your bedroll. I'll roll up my raincoat and use it for a pillow."

He shook his head. "There are two blankets here. We'll share. There's only one pillow. You're welcome to share that, too. If you're still not afraid of me," he added with a bit of mischief.

No, Eve wasn't afraid of him. But how could she trust herself to be so near him? She was afraid to be that close. She was afraid she would feel things that would be unwise and dangerous. She was afraid she would not be able to keep from reaching out and touching his face, his neck, his shoulders, letting her hands run down his muscled arms. Already she wanted him to kiss her. She couldn't let herself want more. He was a stranger. She didn't know him. But already her heart was arguing that point.

"I might snore in your ear," she said, not really knowing what to say. She'd never been in a situation like this. And she'd certainly never been around a man like him before. He was older, sexier, more confident. Something about him told Eve that beneath that fascinating exterior was a man who'd already experienced more than most men would in a whole lifetime.

"I'll reach over and push up your chin," he assured her. "And I'm not worried. I know you won't try to take liberties with me."

She laughed softly as she lay down beside him. "I'll do my best to be perfectly proper."

He switched off the flashlight. The darkness hid the smile on his face. "I hope Rebel doesn't realize you're sleeping in the tent with me. I told him there wasn't room for two in here. His feelings are going to be hurt if he finds out."

Eve listened to him shifting on the bedroll, then felt the pillow move as his head came down a few inches from her.

She was suddenly aware of his warmth and his breath. She pictured his face in the darkness, then swallowed as a faint feeling of suffocation attacked her.

"I won't tell him," she promised.

Eve heard his quiet chuckle next to her. "I knew you would be a woman who didn't sleep and tell."

She smiled faintly and forced her rigid body to relax. He wasn't going to make advances, he wasn't going to take advantage of the situation. He was going to be kind and understanding about the whole thing. Eve was greatly relieved. So why was a tiny part of her let down?

"Thank you, Elliot, for sharing your bed with me."

He shifted to his side, and she knew without seeing that he was facing her. The whole idea made her warm, far too warm.

"It was the only thing a Texas gentleman could do."

She closed her eyes and let out a pent-up breath. He

sounded so relaxed, so laid-back. She wasn't having any kind of effect on him, while he was playing havoc with her whole being.

But then, she reminded herself, she'd never had a great effect on men. Elliot probably liked the glamorous sort, or maybe the petite feminine kind. Maybe there was one in Fort Worth—

Go to sleep, Eve, she told herself. *Go to sleep and forget about this man beside you.*

"Good night, Elliot."

"Good night, Miss Eve."

Chapter Three

Eve awoke with a start. A noise had penetrated the depths of her sleep. Her eyes flew open and her heart thudded.

Disoriented, she raised her head and struggled to remember where she was.

The lake. The fog. Elliot.

It was then she realized her palms were spread flat against his chest, as was most of the rest of her!

"Ssh. It's all right." Elliot's whispered words filled the dark tent. "It's only Rebel rattling our supper plates."

Eve looked over but could not manage to see his face. His hands spanned her waist with a familiarity that shot fire through her veins.

"I—I—I'm sorry, Elliot," she blurted out and quickly made a move to shift away from him.

He reluctantly let her go. "For what?" he asked.

"I—for—forgetting which side of the bed belonged to me."

His smile was hidden by the darkness. "I'm not complaining."

Eve was not prepared for any of this—his words, or the feel of him against her. She had never longed for any man the way she did now, and that longing seemed to have left her paralyzed. She wanted more than anything to slide her palms downward until she found the small nubs of his nipples. She wanted to lean her mouth down to his. To taste the scar on his lip, to know the mystery of his kiss.

"Elliot..." His name came whispering out on her breath.

One of his hands slid slowly up her back until finally it tangled in her hair, then curved against the nape of her neck. His fingers felt strong and rough against her skin, the epitome of the man himself.

"I won't hurt you."

She knew he meant physically. Eve could have told him she wasn't worried about that. She was more concerned about her heart. It was already becoming entangled with this dark, intriguing man, just as her hair was snared between his fingers.

But even knowing this could not stop the downward descent of her head.

As their lips met, Eve felt his hands tighten on her. His lips were hard, warm, compelling her to taste and search out their contours.

Groaning, Elliot shifted them both so that she was lying beneath him. Without breaking the contact with her lips, he caught both her wandering hands and locked his fingers through hers.

She felt small, soft and warm beneath him. When he

drew her arms up over her head, he could feel the movement of her breast against his chest. It was too easy for Elliot to imagine her satiny skin bared to his. The erotic thought brought a pain of hunger to him, making his tongue stab its way between her teeth.

Sensing his urgency, Eve opened her mouth and met his tongue with hers. He tasted wild and wondrous. He tasted of love, and she could not get enough. Heat, heavy and languid, seeped throughout her body. She was lost to him, and her heart and body cried silently for a release into the dark, mysterious place he was leading her to.

His teeth sank into her bottom lip as he released her hands to find the buttons on her blouse. Eve gasped with pleasure as his hands found her breast. She brought her arms up and around his neck, wanting and needing to touch and feel him as he did her.

The faint weight of her slender arms clinging trustingly to him sobered Elliot to some degree. He'd promised not to hurt her, but if he allowed things to go further, he would.

He had a feeling that making love just once to Eve would not be enough for him. That once it happened, she'd be in his life. And he couldn't allow that. His life was shadowed with ugliness, and it would mar her just as it had marred him. She was too gentle, too precious to allow that to happen.

Slowly he levered himself away from her. From a distance he could hear her voice, puzzled, lost.

"Elliot—what is it?"

He breathed deeply, trying to remember when and if his heart had ever galloped like this before. He didn't think so. Not even when he'd been out on the dark city streets, death and danger stalking him like a black ghost. How could one woman do this to him?

"I—" He rubbed a trembling hand over his face, trying to fight the urge to pull her back in his arms. "I— I didn't mean for things to go so far. I meant for it to stop with a kiss."

It took a moment for Eve to realize what he was saying. Still confused, she said, "You weren't the reason it didn't stop. I was—"

"The reason doesn't matter," he quickly put in.

Eve was aching for him. Her breasts felt swollen as she snatched the clothing back across them. It was obvious he regretted what had just occurred. Was there someone else in his life? The idea sliced through her.

"You love someone else." The words rushed out before she could stop them.

The straight-forwardness of her statement jerked his head back around to her. "I love no one."

The sudden, cold bitterness in him amazed Eve. Still, she did not let it stop her. Something had told her almost from the very first that this man would somehow change her life. She believed it even more now.

"Surely you love your mother," she said, forcing her voice to be light, almost teasing.

The heavy tension suddenly seemed to disappear, and she could hear the rush of his sigh. "Yes, my mother," he conceded. "She is the one person I love."

But none other. What did it mean? Only that he simply didn't want her? Eve could hardly believe that. She'd felt the passion in him burning like a bright, beautiful flame. He had wanted her to some degree.

"Then why—"

"Look, Eve, I'm not what you think—I'm not a man

to be getting involved with. You don't know me. You don't want to know me."

"Maybe I should be the judge of that."

He made an impatient sound as he pulled back the flap of the tent and looked out at the night. It was still raining outside. Eve had the impression that if it hadn't been, he would have already left her.

"You don't go around making love to men you don't know."

"I don't go around making love to any man," she corrected.

She hadn't needed to tell him of her innocence. He'd been aware of it from the very start. And he damn sure wasn't going to be the man to end it; he had enough on his mind without that kind of guilt.

"Lie back down and go to sleep, Eve. Nothing is going to happen."

Why, in spite of his words and his sudden aloofness, did she still want to reach out and touch him? "What if I said I wanted it to happen?"

"It wouldn't change anything."

Even though she knew that he was probably right about things, she could not put aside the feelings he produced inside her. He'd stirred her in a way that she'd never felt before. She couldn't just let that slip away without a reason.

"It must be nice to be so self-sufficient, not to need anyone—"

"Don't talk to me about needing! I've needed people before. But you know what?" he asked, his voice growing soft and dangerous. "They all managed to let me down."

Eve winced at the fierceness of his words. Obviously things had not always been good for him, and she'd made him remember that. She didn't know what to say. Meeting him had turned her inside out.

"I'm sorry," she told him after long minutes ticked by.

"Yeah, well, don't feel sorry for me, Eve. I learned long ago that people can't be trusted. Things happen—some get hurt in the process, others go blithely on, not giving a damn one way or the other. It's just the way of life."

She examined his every word before saying, "Do you think I'm one of those people, the ones who don't care?"

"No." He sighed and let the flap of the tent fall shut, enclosing the two of them in a small little world. "I think you're one of those that gets hurt."

Her throat felt tight and achy. She swallowed in an effort to relieve it. "Earlier you said you wouldn't hurt me," she reminded him.

"I'm proving that by not making love to you."

Making love. Yes, that was what it would have been between them. Not just the physical union of two bodies. Maybe it was premature of Eve to be sure of that. Maybe she was reading too much into a few kisses. But her heart didn't think so. She wanted Elliot to know this.

"Elliot...I never felt that way—I mean earlier when we—I never felt that way with anyone. I wanted you to make love to me."

In the darkness, Elliot closed his eyes in torment. Why had this happened? Why had this woman wandered into his camp, turning his emotions topsy-turvy, emotions he'd thought were long dead, better off dead?

"I don't want to hear that," he said. But it was a lie. He did want to hear that he wasn't just another man to her, that he'd affected her just as much as she had him.

"Maybe not. But now you know it anyway," Eve said.

"Go to sleep, Eve. Tomorrow none of this will matter."

The finality of his words stung her. She forced herself to lie down and close her eyes.

It probably wouldn't matter to him, she thought. He'd probably had many women in the past. A few minutes in the arms of another one wouldn't mean much to him. But to Eve it had been like the rising of the sun, and she wondered why fate had brought her to his camp. Why had this night, of all nights, been a white night?

The second time Eve woke, it was to the smell of frying sausage and freshly brewed coffee.

She opened her eyes, saw where she was, then immediately closed them again. She had to go out there and face Elliot. Pretend that last night meant nothing to her.

When she climbed from the tent's small opening, Elliot was by the fire, dishing up scrambled eggs. He was dressed in clean jeans, the same muddy boots and a blue plaid shirt that hung unbuttoned against his brown chest.

"Good morning, Eve," he greeted her.

Their eyes met and she smiled. Seeing him was good, as good as it had been last night. In spite of everything.

"Good morning, Elliot."

She stretched and looked at the sky. Patches of blue were beginning to show through. The fog had dissipated, even though the air hung heavy with moisture. She could go home now. Funny how getting there didn't mean as much to her as it had last night.

"Hope you're hungry. I have breakfast ready."

"I'm very hungry," she assured him.

Eve made another trip to the woods, then sluiced her hands and face with lake water. By the time she returned to camp Elliot had already filled her plate with sausage, eggs and skillet toast.

"It looks like the storm is finally over," she said, taking her plate and joining him by the fire.

"Yes. You'll be able to see your way home now," he told her.

Eve could feel his eyes on her, and she suddenly realized she didn't want to leave him. She knew that once she got home nothing would look the same, and her mind would be on him back here in the woods, alone with his dog.

"Yes, I'll be able to go now."

He didn't say anything, and Eve supposed he would be glad to see her go. She wondered if he was thinking about last night when she'd woken in his arms. She hadn't planned to kiss him like that. She hadn't planned to want him. It had just happened.

"You're a good cook, Elliot. If you ever want to do something besides babysit alligators you can cook in the restaurant."

He grinned faintly as he took up his coffee cup. "I hate to cook. I only do it because my stomach demands it."

She wondered for probably the hundredth time what he really did for a living. "Working within the municipality" hadn't told her much.

"When are you going back to Fort Worth?"

He shrugged negligibly and kept his eyes on his plate. "I don't know. Maybe never."

Eve's eyes widened at his response. He looked like a man who was very sure of himself, so why did he seem to be drifting aimlessly?

"I thought you had a place there?"

"I do."

The impassive answer caused Eve to pull her eyes back to her plate. He was obviously telling her that his life was none of her business.

She quickly finished her coffee and the food on her plate. "Thank you for the breakfast, Elliot. Now I really must be getting home. Since Daddy is gone, someone needs to be there to oversee things."

Elliot watched as she put aside her cup and plate. He'd thought he would be relieved when she left. But now he realized he didn't want her to go. She'd made him realize how empty and lonely his life was. It would be empty again once she left.

His jaw hardened at the thought and he inwardly cursed himself. He could live with that. He'd done it for a long time now. Like Eve had said, he was self-sufficient. He didn't need anyone; especially not a soft little thing like her.

He rose to his feet. "I'll walk you to your boat and make sure you get off safely," he told her.

Eve was surprised at his offer. "That's very kind of you. But I'll be all right."

"Maybe you will. But I want to make sure for myself."

He began to lead the way into the thick woods. Eve followed.

Now that it was daylight, she could see that she had

moored the boat much further from his camp than she'd first thought.

The two of them walked quietly through the tangled underbrush with Rebel at their heels. The rainstorm had left water everywhere. Eve's shoes made a sucking noise in the mud, and the leaves that brushed against her left dark splotches on her clothing.

Once at the boat, Eve tossed her raincoat onto the seat and began to untie the mooring rope.

"Does everything look all right? No leaks or anything stolen?" he asked.

She gave the boat another inspection. "Everything seems fine."

The boat was several feet from shore. So as not to soak her clothing, Eve leaned down and began to roll up the bottom of her jeans. Elliot watched the smooth shapes of her legs come into view until memories of the past night and their shared kisses forced him to look away.

"Well," she said, looking up at him and trying her best to smile. "I guess this is goodbye."

A faint smile settled across his face. "I'm glad you weren't hurt in the fog. I hope you'll never start out across the lake at such a late hour again."

"Don't worry. I've learned my lesson." Her eyes clung to his face, and the touch, the taste, the scent of him burned in her mind. "I hope you'll come to the marina and see me sometime. I'm always there. Will you?"

Would he? No. It wouldn't be wise to see her again. Not wise for either of them. "I don't get out much."

She forced her expression and voice to be light. "Maybe you'd enjoy it if you did. And bring Rebel. Daddy has a penchant for coon dogs."

The old-fashioned idea of meeting her daddy made

him smile. Renea, or any of the other women he'd known in Fort Worth, had been the furthest thing from quaint that he could imagine. Straightforward, cool, unshockable. Those words would better describe them. It was the only kind of woman he'd known. Maybe being two hundred miles east had set him back in time. Or maybe his line of work had limited him to a certain circle of people. He didn't know anymore.

"Maybe. Someday," he told her.

"I'll look for you anyway," she said, then leaned over and cupped his jaw in her hand. "Thank you for sharing your camp, Elliot."

His eyes met hers, and in the morning light she could see the brown, green and gold flecks that made up their hazel color. They were beautiful eyes, and they pulled at something inside her.

"You're welcome, Eve," he said quietly.

Everything about him compelled her to lean forward and kiss him softly on the mouth.

For just a moment, their lips clung, then she pulled away from him and headed purposefully to the boat.

The motor started with little effort, and soon she was backing slowly away from the shore.

Elliot stood there watching her go. Eve, in turn, watched him, Rebel and the bank slip further and further away. Finally she was forced to put the throttle into forward gear.

"Goodbye, Elliot," she called to him.

He lifted a hand in farewell, but Eve could hardly see it. Her eyes were filled with tears.

Pine Ridge Marina was situated on the Texas side of the lake. The block of white buildings trimmed in dark green sat on a wide point of land that jutted into the water like a crooked finger. Towering loblolly pines shaded the lawns and parking area. Azalea bushes scattered across the grounds were in riotous bloom, adding a blaze of color against the greenery.

Eve's father, Burl, kept the buildings in perfect condition, making it one of the finest marinas in the area. Toledo Bend Reservoir was not a recreational lake in all senses of the word. It was filled with too many snags, rotten trees and water moss to be used for skiing or water play. But it was well known for its fishing. Ten to fifteen years ago it had, perhaps, been one of the best fishing lakes in the southern part of the States. Since then, its popularity as easy fishing had dwindled as the population of black bass and crappie was reduced by heavy use.

Still, the marina drew many of the serious, die-hard fishermen, and even some families who merely wanted to enjoy the warm Texas weather. It was enough to keep the family business going.

Burl and Eve lived in a bungalow situated some one hundred yards in back of the motel. From the laundry room, where she was busily folding clothes, Eve could see the lights of the covered boat dock. A man and woman were walking across the wooden ramp that would take them ashore. She could see the orb of their flashlight bobbing against the ground.

She wondered, as she had constantly for the past two days, if Elliot was still at his camp in the woods.

A loud slapping sound against the washing machine made her jump around and squeal with sudden fright. "Daddy! What are you doing home?"

He laughed in the same robust way he lived life.

"They ran me out of Galveston, darlin'. Said the town just wasn't big enough to hold a man like me."

She laughed and promptly went to hug him and kiss his cheek. "And how many women did you leave crying after you?"

"Well, there was this one redhead—"

"Really?"

Burl shook his head, putting a damper on Eve's eager expression. "Not really, honey. I didn't have time for a redhead. The last two days I've looked at enough boats to float half of Texas."

"How did it go? Find anything suitable?"

"You mean did I find anything we could afford? Yes, but it was nothing but junk."

Burl had been planning to purchase several fishing boats in order to start a boat rental service at the marina. He'd already started men working on the construction of another covered boat dock to house the extra boats.

"No luck at all?"

He rubbed a thick hand over his ruddy face. "Well, I wouldn't say that. There's a man coming up Friday to talk business. We might be able to come to some kind of terms."

Eve smiled brightly at this news. She knew how much her father wanted this project to get off the ground. "Oh, how many boats?"

"Five or six. They're used, but in perfect condition. We'll just have to wait and see."

Eve placed the folded clothes in a wicker basket and set it out of the way. Burl curled his arm around his daughter's shoulders and began to lead her toward the kitchen.

"Now, honey girl, tell me everything that's been going on," he urged.

In the kitchen, Eve went about fixing him a glass of iced tea and a sandwich. It was already well past supper. Eve had eaten and cleaned away her mess several hours ago. She smiled as she watched her father devour the roast beef sandwich.

"The same old thing has been going on. The motel and restaurant have been very busy. The ice machine broke down, but Bob got it going again. Just a loose wire or something."

"Has he kept the men working on the dock?"

She nodded at her father's mention of Bob, his friend and coworker. "I walked down before the men quit work this evening. It's looking great."

Burl sighed with obvious relief. "Thank goodness. All the while I was in Galveston I had the oddest feeling that something wasn't quite right up here. I'm glad to hear my hunch was wrong. You've been all right, have you? Not feeling puny?"

She smiled at him, knowing he loved her excessively. "A healthy thing like me? I'm feeling wonderful," she assured him.

Eve was forced to look away from her father as she spoke the last words, because they were only partially true. Physically she did feel fine. But mentally she'd felt very torn the past two days. Elliot was never out of her mind, and she didn't know what to do about it.

She kept telling herself that he was just a man that she'd crossed paths with along the way. He didn't want anything to do with her, and she'd be better off to forget him. But she was finding that forgetting him was an impossible thing to do.

His kiss, his touch, the lines on his face, the color of his eyes were etched in her memory and refused to go away.

"Evie? I said, are we booked yet for the weekend?"

Eve looked back at her father, a blank expression on her face. "Sorry, Daddy, I was thinking about something."

"That much was obvious," he said, pushing his empty plate back. Folding his hands across his chest, he leaned back in the chair and gave her a thoughtful look.

"Did something happen around here that you're not telling me about?"

Leave it to her father to be so observant. "Well, no. I did get stranded in the boat coming back from Zwolle in the fog, but I made it home okay."

Eve wasn't going to say any more than that. Even though she was twenty-five years old, her father wouldn't take a kind view of her sleeping in a tent with a strange man. Even if it had been an unusual situation.

Burl accepted her answer, although his snort let her know he didn't like the idea of her being out in the boat alone. "I've told you about being out by yourself like that, girl. From now on you take the pickup, you hear me?"

"Yes, Daddy. I will," she promised. If she'd been in the pickup three nights ago, she would have never met Elliot, and she wouldn't be consumed with thoughts of him now. But to take away that night would be like taking her breath away, she realized.

Chapter Four

The weekend proved to be very busy. Crappie were the big catch at this time of the year, and the fishermen were out in force. The motel was full, and the restaurant was busy from dawn to ten o'clock at night.

Throughout Eve's busy workdays, she often looked up to search for Elliot's face among the crowd. She hoped that he would change his mind and decide he would like to see her again. Yet by the time another week had passed, Eve decided he wasn't going to show up at Pine Ridge. That left her with only one choice: she would go to see him.

Wednesday of the next week proved to be a slack day at the marina. Early that morning Eve set about making a blackberry cobbler.

Once it was out of the oven and cooling, she changed into a fresh pair of blue jeans, a pair of brown boots and a white shirt. After a dab of lipstick, mascara and the flip of a hairbrush, she grabbed the cobbler and headed out the door before she could change her mind.

Her newly washed hair bounced around her shoulders as she walked toward the faded blue pickup parked beneath the carport. Some five years ago, her dad had declared the Ford hers. It was like a familiar pet to her now. Her brother called her sentimental for holding on to it; she called herself practical.

It was a fair, hot day. Birds chattered in the pines above her head, and down on the new boat dock the noise of hammers and saws carried the sound of progress. She felt good. She was going to see Elliot. Right or wrong, to Eve that was progress.

"Going somewhere, Evie?"

Eve was just about to start the motor when the sound of her father's voice stopped her. Glancing out the window, she saw him approaching the pickup.

"Yes. For a visit of sorts."

The big, redheaded man drew a kerchief from his pants pocket and proceeded to wipe the sweat from his face.

"Glad to hear it. You've been needing a rest from this place. Who you going to see?"

Eve had never lied to her father. She might leave out a few details sometimes, but she'd never deliberately lied to him. She didn't intend to start now, even though she sensed that he would disapprove of her being interested in a man like Elliot.

"I don't think you'd know him. He's from Fort Worth. I—I met him over by Zwolle the other night."

This put an interested look on Burl's broad features. "You met a man."

She chuckled at his surprise. "Why, yes, Daddy. I do

meet men sometimes. Even though you think you're going to have an old maid on your hands."

"Hell, girl, I'm not worried about that. I'm more concerned about some man coming along and breaking that soft little heart of yours."

"This one won't. He's not the least bit interested in me," she said, then smiled as her father began to scowl.

"Sounds like a damn fool to me. What are you wasting your time going to see him for?"

Eve had asked herself the same question over and over ever since she'd decided to make this trip. She hadn't found the answer to it yet.

"Don't worry," she said with a wry smile. "He's the Marshalls' grandson. You remember them?"

He thought for a moment. "Yeah, I remember. Good people. But I don't remember any boy."

Eve started the engine while thinking how amusing it was to hear Elliot described as a boy. What would her father think if he ever did see him?

"Well, don't worry, anyway," she told him.

He grimaced and waved her away. But Eve caught the fond twinkle for her in his eyes.

"Get out of here. I got work to do," he growled.

The dirt road that led to the Marshall place ran for at least five miles off the main highway. Eve drove slowly through the pine woods, trying to decide what she would say to him once she got there.

However, words weren't necessary once she reached the old homestead. No one was there. She knew it the moment she pulled to a stop in front of the wooden fence.

Rebel would have been out barking. And wherever Elliot was, that was where the hound would be.

She climbed slowly out of the truck and entered the yard. The grass needed mowing, and blackberry vines were threatening to cover one end of the fence. There was nothing on the wide wooden porch or in the yard that would have led her to believe anyone lived there. It was merely an old house, surrounded by woods that were threatening to overrun it.

Bird song was the only thing to be heard as she walked across the porch and knocked on the screen door.

"Elliot, are you here?"

She tried the door and found it locked. Disappointment swamped her, and she started back to the truck. Halfway there she remembered the cobbler and wondered what she was going to do with it. She wanted Elliot to have it, but she wasn't about to leave it sitting on the porch. A dog or some wild animal would have it torn apart by the time he found it.

A thought struck her, and she turned and made her way around to the back of the house. A wide, screened-in porch was connected to the back of the house.

Eve walked up the steps and tried the back door. It was open. She peered around it and into the kitchen. The room was clean except for a dirty TV dinner tray left on the cabinet counter.

He must have told the truth about not liking to cook, she thought wryly. She could imagine him sitting and eating alone at the table. Did he like it that way? She hated thinking he might be lonely.

Back at the pickup she fished out a pen and piece of paper from her purse. She wrote:

Dear Elliot,
I came for a visit. I thought you might like the cobbler, even though it's not nearly as good as what your grandmother baked.

I'm still waiting for you to come to the marina to see me. I hope you will.

Eve

She carried the note and the pic around to the back porch and placed it on the end of the cabinets just inside the kitchen door.

On the drive home Eve wondered how long it would be before he came home and found the note. How long, if ever, would it be before she saw him again?

It was well after dark when Elliot returned home in his Jeep. Behind the seat was the tent, food and camping gear. He'd packed up his camp some two hours ago and now Rebel sat in the seat opposite him, his tongue lolling out, his brown eyes questioning.

"I know, Rebel," Elliot told the dog. "I've stopped the Jeep. It's time to get out. You don't have to remind me."

Rebel's tail thumped against the seat. Elliot shoved up the door handle, then slid to the ground with the dog quickly following.

It was a hot, sultry evening, and Elliot was in a foul mood. He wanted a cold beer and a hot bath. And he wanted to quit thinking about Eve Crawford.

It took a few minutes for him to unload the camping gear from the back of the Jeep. While he worked, Rebel began to sniff out a trail leading from the back porch around to the front yard.

His excited yelps brought a wry grin to Elliot's face. He was glad that at least one of them had some enthusiasm.

"Did a rabbit have the nerve to walk across your yard?" he asked the hound.

The question only encouraged Rebel to bark louder. He kept up the baying all through Elliot's trips to and from the Jeep and the porch.

Elliot wondered if a possum or coon had decided to den up under the house, but he was too tired to look.

A few minutes later, after all the gear was stored away, Elliot discovered what Rebel had been trying to tell him. The dog had scented female, and that female had been Eve.

Elliot stood in the middle of the kitchen, his eyes going from the note to the pie. It would have surprised him to discover just a note, but the cobbler along with it amazed him.

The smell of it filled the kitchen, and for just a moment or two he envisioned this place as it had been years before. His grandmother standing at the stove, his grandfather sitting at one end of the table, packing his pipe with tobacco. Good smells and good laughter had filled the whole house then. It had been the only "home" he'd ever had. But time marched on in spite of everything. He'd watched his grandfather slip away, and then his grandmother soon followed.

Now, even with Elliot in it, the place seemed empty.

Empty. He hated the word. It had popped up regularly since he'd met Eve Crawford. It was strange how one woman like her could remind him of good things and bad things.

He picked up the note and read it for a second time. This time the corners of his mouth lifted ever so slightly. Elliot could picture her writing it, her graceful fingers carefully forming the words.

Lifting the note to his nose, he sniffed, expecting the

scent of roses he associated with her to be on the paper, too. But it wasn't. It smelled like a plain piece of paper.

Hell, Elliot, getting sentimental isn't your style. And it's too late to change now. He stuffed the note in his shirt pocket. Out of sight, out of mind, he told himself.

Deciding he'd dig into the pie later, he crossed to the refrigerator and rummaged around on the bottom shelf for a long-necked bottle of beer. He twisted off the cap, threw it in the trash, then drank half the contents as he headed to the bathroom.

Nothing had changed in the house since it had first been built. The bathroom fixtures were as old as everything else. Elliot sat down on the edge of the claw-footed tub and began to tug off his crusty boots. He sat the beer carefully to one side, but still within reach.

The water system consisted of a well with a small electrical pump. The pressure was rather poor, but Elliot didn't mind. It was clean and hot and wet. That was all that mattered to him.

Moments later, as the warm water seeped into his tired muscles, he swigged the beer and allowed himself to think about Eve's note.

On different occasions in the past, women had pursued him. He knew all the signs, and he knew how to dodge them when he wanted to. But Eve was a different matter altogether. He knew she wasn't the type to go after a man. He doubted that a notion like that had ever entered her head.

No, coming to see him had been a much simpler thing for her. She'd done it because she liked him as a person, she'd wanted to do something for him, and she'd wanted to see him again. There was no guile about her. And that was new to Elliot.

Impulsively he leaned over and fished the note from his shirt pocket. *I'm still waiting for you to come to the marina to see me,* he read again.

He thought once more of how she'd felt in his arms, how sweet her lips had tasted. His hands had shaken as he'd told her things couldn't go any further. Something about their coming together had stirred more than his body.

The idea left him groaning, and he slid further beneath the water until it lapped against his shoulders. Eve Crawford could just keep waiting to see him, he thought determinedly. If he wanted a woman, he'd go back to Fort Worth and find one of his own kind. One without strings and attachments, one that would get up from his bed the next morning, say goodbye and go blithely on her way.

A few minutes later, the beer bottle and the tub were both empty. Elliot, barefoot and dressed in an old pair of Levi's and white T-shirt, was sitting at the kitchen table. He'd just finished a bowl of the blackberry cobbler. It had tasted even better than he had anticipated, and he wondered if Eve or one of the restaurant cooks had made it.

With a sigh he tilted back the wooden chair and linked his fingers at the back of his neck. The house had no air-conditioning. Elliot had opened all the windows, but there was very little breeze to be felt. He was already sweating. And besides being hot, the house seemed unbearably quiet.

There was an old black and white TV in the living room, but he wasn't a TV person. He liked the radio, but he wasn't in the mood for music.

Restlessly he rose from the table and walked to the open screen door. Rebel was stretched out on the wooden floor of the porch, his sides rapidly rising and falling from the oppressive heat.

Elliot had gotten the dog as soon as he'd come back to east Texas. Rebel had been with him through the long past months and had become Elliot's only companion. The dog had proved to be far more faithful than any human he'd ever known.

Back at the table Elliot filled his bowl with more pie and carried it out to the porch.

"Here, boy, dig in," he told the dog, setting the bowl down in the front of his nose.

Rebel went after the treat with quick thoroughness. Elliot watched the dog lick his chops with appreciation.

He'd heard more than once that you weren't supposed to give a dog sweets, but he wasn't a man who followed the rules. Life would be too dull that way.

Bending the rules was something Elliot had done all his life. And even though that kind of living had gotten him into trouble on occasion, he knew he wouldn't change his way of thinking. He'd never bent them to hurt anyone, and he'd never bent them for his own personal gain. If that still made him guilty, then so be it.

The past seven months had not changed his way of thinking. Seven more wouldn't, either. He did things his way, he lived life his way. It was the only way for Elliot.

He stroked Rebel's head then walked back into the kitchen. Unable to stop himself, he pulled open a drawer in the cabinet. Lying to one side of the silverware was a .38 Special strapped in a leather holster.

Elliot pulled the pistol from the worn leather and

snapped the cylinder from the firing mechanism. Then, holding it up to the light, he gave a flip of thumb and watched the empty chambers spin around in a harmless circle.

No, he thought grimly. He wouldn't change. And that meant a woman like Eve had no place in his life. It was that simple, wasn't it?

"I've decided to keep the barbecue ribs for the Saturday night special."

Eve looked over at the woman standing at the long cooking grill. She was in her early forties, a bit plump, and had a kind, round face. Because she was cooking, her blond hair was crushed beneath a fine hair net.

"That's fine with me, Marcia. I think the customers have started looking forward to it. And we might lose them if we change the ribs to something else," Eve told her as she chopped cabbage on a wide cutting board.

It was a little before four o'clock. The evening diners would arrive soon. The staff tried to have the buffet table ready by five. Eve usually worked here and there, wherever she was needed the most. Tonight was catfish and hush puppy night, so Eve was helping with the coleslaw. Another girl, Cora, would come on duty after four. Presently there was only Eve, Marcia and a waitress, Faye, working.

"Did I tell you Herb took me out to dinner last night?" Marcia asked.

Eve looked thoughtfully over at her friend and co-worker. "No, what was the occasion?"

"Our twenty-eighth wedding anniversary," Marcia proudly announced. She turned away from the grill and the frying hamburger meat and walked across to the opposite counter where Eve was still chopping cabbage.

"Can you believe we've been married that long?"

The two women had been friends for years. Marcia had worked for the Crawfords ever since they first opened the marina restaurant.

"With your temper? It's incredible," Eve teased.

"A temper! Me? Herb's middle name is temper."

"You're crazy about the guy," Eve said, speaking of Marcia's husband.

Marcia laughed and went quickly back to the grill and flipped over the hamburger patty. "Yeah, I am. We had a lovely time, too. He even ordered a bottle of wine, and we talked for hours."

"Oooh, that sounds romantic," Eve agreed, glad to hear her friend had had a nice evening. She deserved it. She was a hard worker and a dedicated wife and mother to her family.

Marcia gave Eve a droll look. "I'm surprised you think that. I've given up on you being romantic."

"Marcia, I've had my share of boyfriends. Just because I don't go out all the time, you think it's a crime."

The older woman began to slather mustard on a warm bun. "What I think is a crime is for a woman as beautiful as you not to have a man in her life. A permanent one."

Eve pursed her lips and chopped harder. "Marcia, you know I intend to go to college. That's going to take up a big part of my attention. And if and when I ever get married, I want it to be permanent. I want to make sure I'm getting the right man for me. So how did you know Herb was the one?"

Marcia finished putting the hamburger together, placed it on a thick white plate, then dumped a pile of french fries next to it. "There's just a feeling inside you that lets you know. I don't know how to explain it. I was only fifteen when we got married, but I knew."

She put the plate on the pickup shelf and dinged a bell beside it.

"Well, obviously you knew right. You and Herb are like two peas in a pod."

"Guess we are," Marcia agreed with a sly smile. "He still makes me feel wonderful and furious, happy and sad, all the things that go with loving. But you'll know this someday—if you ever start looking," she added dryly.

Eve raked the pile of chopped cabbage into a plastic bowl. Marcia's words had her thinking of Elliot. She'd tried these past few days to put him out of her mind, but it hadn't worked. He was still there, taunting her with his memory. She wondered if he'd found her note and the pie. She'd wanted to drive back and see for herself, but had told herself it would be too forward of her to do such a thing.

"I have a law career to think of," Eve said.

"Is that going to keep you warm and contented?"

"A man isn't everything," Eve countered.

"Neither is a career," Marcia quipped.

Eve sighed as she pictured Elliot's face in the firelight, his mouth lifting with a faint smile. Why did she miss him so? "I want to get my degree. Do something with my life."

Marcia wiped her hands against the white apron that was wrapped around her. "That's all well and good, honey. But it would be nice to be loved along the way, too."

Eve was watching a basket of frying hush puppies when Faye hurriedly pushed through the swinging doors of the kitchen.

She was a tall, slim black woman with beautiful high cheekbones and a never-ending smile. Eve was as close to Faye as she was to Marcia. Both women were probably the dearest friends she had.

"These are almost ready, Faye. Do you need them now?"

Faye's smile grew even wider. "No, I need you."

Eve's eyes widened. The restaurant usually had a pretty good crowd on Friday night, but Faye was always able to handle the tables. "Are we that busy?" She looked around for Marcia, but found the kitchen empty. Sighing, she glanced down at the browning clumps of cornbread. "They'll just have to wait until I dump these."

"I don't mean to wait on tables," Faye said. "There's someone out there who wants to see you."

The hush puppies appeared to be done. Eve lifted the huge basket from the frying well and dumped them into a loaf pan lined with paper towels.

"But I'm busy, Faye. Is it important?"

Faye dimpled saucily and turned her palms upward. "I'd call this guy important any time of the day."

Eve slowly turned her eyes on Faye. "Did you say guy?"

"I sure did."

Her heart thumping, Eve began to fumble with the pan of hush puppies. "What did he look like?"

Faye waved her hand through the air and laughed. "Who has time to stand around gawking? I'd say he looks all man to me."

Obviously Faye hadn't seen him before. That could only mean—was it really him?

Faye winked and began to hurry away. "I'll tell him you'll be right out," she called back to Eve.

The dining area of the restaurant consisted of one long room with plate glass on two sides. Along these walls were booths covered with deep green vinyl trimmed in beige, and in the middle were coordinating tables and chairs.

At one end of the room were the entrance and the cashier's stand. It was there that Eve spotted him. He was standing to one side of the doors, a pair of wire-framed sunglasses dangling from his hand.

Happiness burst inside her at the sight of him. She hurried through the maze of tables and diners, her smile growing with each step she took.

Halfway across the room, he spotted her, and one side of his mouth lifted in a faint grin of acknowledgement.

Once she reached him, she clasped both his hands and gave them a quick squeeze. "Elliot, I'm so glad you came."

"It looks like I picked a bad time," he said. "You're busy and—"

"Don't be silly. Faye and Marcia are seeing after things," she assured him. "Come on, would you like to eat?"

She put her hand on his arm and urged him along the wall toward an empty booth. Along the way she noticed he was dressed in a pair of Levi's and a white shirt with short sleeves. The mud had been cleared from his boots, and he wore a watch on his wrist. However, the stubble on his face was at least three days old, and his hair had grown even longer than when she'd seen him last. But neither of these two things distracted from his looks. To Eve there was only one word to describe him: magnificent.

"I really didn't come to eat," he explained. "I was just driving back from Center and thought I'd stop by—"

"Nonsense. Of course you want to eat. I haven't eaten yet. And tonight is catfish night," she told him. "Do you like catfish?"

He slid into one side of the booth and grinned up at her. "Did you cook it?"

She smiled back at him, thinking how wonderful it was to see him again, how much she'd longed for this moment to happen.

"Part of it. Now just stay put and I'll bring us two plates. Tea or coffee?"

"Coffee," he said.

Eve hurried away to the buffet table and grabbed an empty tray.

"Thought you were busy," Faye teased alongside Eve's ear.

"I'm even busier now," Eve replied, beginning to fill two plates with food.

"Who is he?" Faye asked curiously.

"I'll tell you later. Can you manage things without me?"

Faye winked. "I'll make sure we can," she told Eve, then hurried off to take care of a customer.

When Eve returned to the booth with their food, Elliot was gazing out the plate glass that looked out over the boat docks and lake. His expression was pensive, and Eve wondered who or what he was thinking of.

"Beautiful view, isn't it?" Eve asked as she carefully placed his plate in front of him. "I think it's one of our main attractions. The pines, the lake, the lights twinkling like stars in the water."

"It's beautiful," he agreed, watching her as she took the seat opposite him.

She reached around her back and began to untie her

apron. Once she had the strings loose, she pulled it over her head and laid it in the booth beside her.

A pale blue blouse came into his view, and Elliot's eyes were drawn to the V-neck that ended at the top of her cleavage. Her skin was creamy and damp with sweat, as were the tendrils of dark hair that framed her face. He realized he had missed her these past two weeks. More than he cared to admit.

"So, you've been to Center. Anything exciting going on over there?"

He shook his head and reached for his fork. "Not that I saw." He looked across the table and met her gray eyes. "Thank you for the cobbler, Eve. It was nice of you to bring it out."

"There's nothing nice about blackmail," she told him. "I only took it to you to try and draw you out of the woods."

He smiled lazily at her. "I don't believe that."

She laughed softly. "No, it wasn't blackmail. I brought it out because I thought you might enjoy it."

He sliced into a piece of the flaky catfish. "You were right, I did. So did Rebel."

Her brows lifted. "Oh, so Rebel likes blackberry cobbler, too. I'm glad I fixed something you both enjoyed. Were you still at the camp that day?"

He nodded while chewing the fish and watching her dig hungrily into the food on her plate. "I packed up and came in that evening. The gators seemed to be doing all right by themselves."

"What about your friend? The one who works for the department of wildlife?"

"I'm sure he's happy because I haven't run across any poachers." He kept his eyes on her face. He'd pictured it often in his mind these past couple of weeks.

Now he knew he hadn't misjudged her beauty. "The food is delicious. I see why the place is so busy."

His compliment left her feeling warm and glad. "I have good help."

"And where do you fit in?"

"Anywhere I'm needed." She bit into a hush puppy and felt her cheeks grow warm as his eyes continued to study her face. He looked at her as no man had before. It was not a bold or vulgar look, but rather a strange mixture of tenderness and sexiness. It constantly reminded Eve she was a woman.

"So, what have you been doing with yourself? Rescuing more stranded women?"

Elliot laughed softly. "No. You must be the only adventuress around here."

"You're being kind, Elliot. Daddy would call me a foolish woman instead of an adventuress."

He lifted his coffee cup and took a long drink before he asked, "Was your father out hunting for you when you got home?"

Eve shook her head. "He was still in Galveston, thank goodness. He'd have had a fit."

"Because of me?" he asked, a wry twist to his mouth.

She laughed and shook her head. "Daddy will like you. You'll stay and meet him, won't you?"

"I doubt he'd be interested."

"Don't bet on it."

Elliot chuckled, and he suddenly realized he was glad he'd come to see her. She made him feel good and special. She made him feel like a man again.

They finished up their meal with a piece of lemon pie and coffee, then Eve caught Faye and Marcia in the kitchen to ask if they needed her help any longer. Both women looked at Eve as if they wanted to kill her for even asking, so Eve scrambled back to the front to join Elliot.

"They insist they no longer need me," she told him. "So why don't we go outside and I'll show you around the grounds."

"Let me pay for the meal first," he said, reaching around to draw his wallet from his jeans pocket.

Eve hastily caught his arm. "I wouldn't take anything. You're my guest. Besides, you fed me two meals the other day. I still owe you one."

He saw the determination on her face and jammed the wallet back in his jeans. "Now you'll think I came just to get a free meal."

"No, I won't," she said, linking her arm through his and leading him outside. "I'll think you came because I asked you to."

She would be right, Elliot thought. He had come because she had asked, and because in the end he couldn't stop himself from wanting to see her again.

It was a beautiful night. The hot day had cooled down enough to give a balmy feel to the air. Earlier in the evening, Eve had been tired from standing most of the day. But now that Elliot had come she'd forgotten all about the ache in her legs.

"Let's go down by the docks," she suggested, "Daddy just purchased boats to rent. They arrived only yesterday."

Yard lights burned here and there to cast a faint glow on the walkways. She looked up at him as they began to stroll along. "Did you bring Rebel?"

"He's in the back of the Jeep. I told him to stay put."

"For heaven's sake, call him and get him out of there. I'm sure he'd like to come along, too," Eve said.

Elliot gave a shrill whistle, and in less than thirty seconds Rebel was bounding up to them. The dog hadn't forgotten Eve. He barked excitedly and circled her twice.

Eve laughed and kneeled down to kiss the pretty hound on the nose. "You gorgeous thing," she crooned to the dog.

Elliot watched her dote on Rebel and tried to imagine Renea kissing Rebel's wet nose, but it was just too impossible.

"Is this where you've always lived?" he asked Eve.

She shook her head as they continued down a sloping path to the docks.

"No. When I was small we lived in New Orleans. Daddy worked on a shrimp boat. But that was a long time ago."

"Is that where you were born?"

She nodded. "Mama died there. She stepped off a curb and a truck hit her. We still don't know why she didn't see it coming. I really hate that I can't separate her death from the city. It always ruins my visits there."

"I can see why it would. Have you ever been to Fort Worth?"

"No. Never had any reason to. What's it like?"

He shrugged. "Hot and sprawling. Like most of Texas."

"Do you have lots of friends there? I guess you do," she went on without waiting for his answer. "That's where you lived."

"A few." He didn't want to tell her that many of them had quit being his friend. That there were only two or three left who still called him a friend.

"Do you miss it?"

"Fort Worth? No, I try not to think of it."

What a strange comment, Eve thought. She started to ask him why, but by now they were at the dock.

Rebel bounded ahead of them, trotting across the planked floor and sniffing curiously over the edge of the lake water.

"Do you ever fish?" she asked him.

The past years he'd worked so many hours a week that sleep was about all he'd had time for on his off hours. At the time it had seemed normal. Any other kind of life would have been strange to Elliot.

Seven months of near solitude had allowed him a lot of thinking time. And now he could see that his life had always narrowed down to one thing: his work. Maybe that was where he'd gone wrong. Maybe he'd tried too hard.

"I haven't fished since I was a kid," he said quietly.

The two of them walked slowly out on the floating dock. It weaved slightly beneath the movement of their feet. Elliot reached out and spread a steadying hand at the back of Eve's waist.

"Maybe I should take you some time. I know a few good fishing holes. You could put the catch in the freezer. Rebel might like a fish supper once in a while," she said with an impish smile for him.

He looked at her, a teasing glint in his eyes. "You mean you'd guarantee a catch?"

"Of course. My father runs a marina. It would be pretty embarrassing if I couldn't."

"Hmm. A confident woman, aren't you?"

She smiled as she cherished the feel of his hand against her. "Sometimes. When I know my subject."

They strolled down the aisle between the boats until they reached the end. Eve sat down on the bow of a boat and looked up at him as he stood there beside her. From the moment she'd seen him standing in the restaurant, she'd been wondering what his visit really meant.

"I've looked for you these past two weeks. I was about to decide that you weren't coming," she said.

His eyes lowered until they finally slipped away from her. "Right up until an hour ago I told myself not to. It didn't do any good."

Eve's heart lurched forward. "I'm glad it didn't. Because I've missed you."

He gave her a sidelong glance that eventually turned into a grin. "Are you always so frank, Eve?"

Since they'd shared their kisses in his tent the other night, he'd dropped the formal Miss from her name. Eve was pleased to think that he considered them closer than that now.

"I don't believe in hemming and hawing," she told him.

He stepped closer and reached for her hands. With a gentle tug he pulled her to her feet until she was standing before him, inches between their faces. "Neither do I, Eve."

Chapter Five

Eve's eyes locked with Elliot's, and a spasm of awareness shook her. He wanted her. It was there on his face and in his eyes. And no one had to explain to Eve the warmth of desire spreading through her.

Wordlessly Elliot's head moved downward. Eve's lashes slowly fell, her chin tilted upward with languid anticipation.

When their lips finally met, it was like a sweet reacquaintance, and more. Eve lifted her arms and circled them around his neck. Elliot pulled her close, wrapping his arms around her slender form in a possessive grip.

For the past two weeks, Eve had relived his kisses over and over. She'd craved them, dreamed of them, fantasized that this would happen again. Now that it was happening, she was sure the dock was tilting dangerously beneath her feet.

"I've missed you, Eve," he murmured, breaking his lips away from hers.

"Is that why you stayed away?" she whispered.

His mouth brushed back and forth against her neck. Eve felt weak as goosebumps broke out along her arms and down her spine.

"I've stayed away because I knew this would happen," he said huskily.

Eve started to speak, but he covered her mouth once again. This time his kiss was hungry and searching. She clung to him, certain that everything around them was slipping further and further away. She felt his hands slide up her ribs, across her back and finally around her breast. She marveled that his touching her should feel so right, so good.

She was breathless when Elliot finally broke the kiss. For long moments they looked at each other, each trying to uncover what was behind the other's eyes.

"You don't want this to happen between us." She said it as a statement, not a question.

Elliot said, "A part of me doesn't. The other part wants it like hell."

Eve shook her hair away from her face, then lifted her head back in order to see him. "Why?"

His hands came up to frame her face. Eve watched his eyes close as his thumbs reached out and stroked across her cheeks.

The sensual touch evoked a quiver deep inside Eve. She slid her arms around his waist and unashamedly pressed herself against him.

"Because you're not my type of woman," he said.

His raw, husky voice told Eve he was as affected by

her as she was by him. But his words contradicted his body's response to her.

"You type your women, like blood?"

Elliot opened his eyes as a sexy grin spread across his mouth. "I guess your next question will be what type I've categorized you as."

She smiled and breathed in deeply. It was such a heady thing to be in his arms. "I already know my type. A plus."

He chuckled and pulled her head close against his chest. "It makes me feel good to be with you, Eve. Did you know that?"

She rubbed her cheek against him, thinking how she liked the way his hands felt in her hair. "I only know what it feels like for me to be with you. Nice. Very nice."

He held her tight for a few more moments. Eve could hear the strong, steady beat of his heart and feel the shallow rise and fall of his chest. She thought she could stand there forever in his arms and be insanely happy.

Finally he put her away from him but still held on to both her hands. Eve hadn't known that holding hands could be a sensual experience until Elliot locked them intimately together.

"You may not think that, once you get to know me," he said.

She looked into his eyes. "If you were so sure of that, then why did you show up here tonight?"

He looked at her a moment, as if he needed to measure his words carefully. "Because I couldn't quit thinking about you. Because I wanted to kiss you again. Because I'm a damn idiot," he growled with a bit of regret.

Eve wondered why he should have such mixed

emotions. Had some woman burned him in the past? Or was he just a man who didn't like to get involved with women, didn't like commitments of any sort?

"For being attracted to me? Thanks, Elliot. You are a Texas gentleman," she said in a dry, teasing way.

One side of his mouth cocked upward. "I've been called much worse."

"You won't stay away anymore, will you?"

"If I really wanted to be good to you, I would."

She shook her head. "I thought when a man was attracted to a woman, he went after her."

"Obviously you haven't been involved with very many men."

"That's true," she confessed. "Would you have been happier if I were an experienced woman?"

He sighed. "No, Eve. I like you as you are."

This was enough to make Eve happy, and she smiled at him. "And I like you as you are, Elliot. See how simple it is?"

He laughed, and for the first time in months his heart lifted. He wasn't dead after all. Eve was bringing him back to life. Now all he had to do was decide where he wanted that life to go.

"You make things seem that way," he told her.

Her fingers tightened against his. "They are, Elliot," she whispered. "Give me the chance and I'll prove it to you."

"I told myself I didn't even like women anymore. Now I wish you were going home with me. You have me mixed up, Eve."

He wasn't the only one, she thought. "Maybe that's good. Sometimes people need mixing up."

He grinned, and Eve studied the white line of his teeth. The image reminded her of the erotic feel of him biting her lip. The mere memory of it caused a stirring deep inside her.

"Would you go home with me if I asked you to?"

The question was as provocative as the feel of his thighs pressed against hers. Eve had never wanted to give herself to any man—until Elliot. Still, she knew it was too soon, and somehow she knew, as she had that night in the woods, that there would be more involved than just a physical union if she ever agreed.

"What would you do if I said yes?"

He'd probably shake like hell, he thought, but he'd do his best not to let her know it. "Why don't you try it and see?" he invited.

Eve laughed softly, a sound that Elliot found distinctly sexy. "It took you two weeks just to come to the marina to see me. I can't see you carting me off to bed an hour later."

Elliot could damn well see it, but he could hardly let Eve know that. She wasn't a woman who would give her affection lightly, and he wondered, as he had several times in the past hour, what he was doing there. What was he doing with Eve? She wasn't the kind of woman he needed!

"Not that you'd go," he said offhandedly.

Eve breathed deeply. "Not that I'd go," she echoed.

The tension between them was suddenly tangible. Elliot's body was reacting to her soft breast pushed against his chest, her hips and thighs warm and maddeningly feminine against the length of his legs.

"Well, uh, maybe we'd better go see your daddy," he suggested. "It's late and I need to be getting home."

It wasn't all that late, but Eve knew he was using the excuse to end the physical thing between them that seemed to be growing out of control with each passing moment.

Eve didn't disagree with him, although a part of her wanted to. "Yes, maybe you're right," she said, her eyes quietly telling him that she still wanted him anyway.

Elliot had to stifle a groan of frustration as he curved an arm around her shoulders and guided her off the dock.

Eve's father, Burl, was in the kitchen of their bungalow going over a mound of paperwork. The older man's expression held a hint of surprise when Eve showed Elliot into the room.

His daughter's face was glowing warmly as she introduced the two men. "Elliot is the Marshalls' grandson. You remember me mentioning him to you?"

"Of course I do," Burl said, rising up from his chair to grip Elliot's offered hand. "Nice to meet you, Elliot. Are you enjoying your stay here on the lake?"

"It's not as pleasant as it was when my grandparents were still alive, but it's been enjoyable. Not at all like the big city."

Burl laughed. "No, we take things pretty slow around here. Too slow for many people's taste. But I like it that way." Burl looked at his daughter. "Fix us some coffee, darlin'. I'll bet Elliot would like a cup, wouldn't you, son?"

"Thank you, I would like that," Elliot agreed, and pulled out a chair at the chrome-and-blue formica table.

While Elliot took his seat, Burl pushed his paperwork aside. Across the room, Eve busied herself getting the coffee fixings.

Elliot looked at Eve's father. It had been a long time since anyone had called him son. He'd felt old for a long time, and it amazed him that Burl didn't see him as old. Still, the family connotation of the word made him feel warm and welcome.

"You have a nice place here, Mr. Crawford. It must take a lot of work to keep everything going."

"It does," Burl agreed with a proud grin. "But the Pine Ridge is kinda like a child to me now. I wouldn't know what to do with myself if I didn't have it to take care of."

"You'd have me to take care of, Daddy," Eve pointed out as she carried the coffee over to the two men.

"Bull," Burl scoffed. "You haven't needed to be taken care of in a long time." He turned his eyes on Elliot. "She's independent as hell sometimes. Most women are these days, I guess. She wants to be a lawyer. I told her fine, but she'd better learn to pack a gun, because she's damn well gonna make a lot of enemies."

Eve sighed. It was no secret that her father wasn't wild about her decision to go to law school. He was from the old school and believed a woman's place was in the home. "You'll be happy to know that Elliot agrees with you. He's already told me I won't be happy being a prosecutor."

The older man looked at Elliot with new regard. "I know an intelligent man when I see one. You should listen to a pair of smart men, Evie."

Eve shook her head and laughed good-naturedly. "If either one of you gets into trouble and needs a lawyer, I hope the state appoints you a good one, because I'll be on the other side."

Burl laughed. Elliot merely sat there. Eve studied him from beneath her lashes and wondered what was behind his guarded expression.

"So, son, what do you do back in Fort Worth?" Burl asked.

Elliot didn't say anything at first, and Eve began to

wonder if he was going to totally ignore her father's question.

"I'm in between jobs right now. But I did work for the city."

Burl's rusty-colored eyebrows lifted curiously. "You looking for a job around here?"

Elliot shrugged. "I don't know yet. I haven't decided if I'm staying or not."

Burl looked over at Eve, and she didn't have to second-guess her father's expression. He wasn't pleased at all with Elliot's evasive attitude.

She glowered back at her father until Burl finally looked away from his daughter and turned his attention back to his coffee.

"Elliot's been babysitting alligators," Eve told her father. "He has a friend in the wildlife department over in Louisiana."

"Run into any poachers?" Burl asked.

"A couple of months ago. But not recently."

"I hope you kicked their butts. I hate poachers. Law breakers of the lowest kind, if you ask me."

Elliot's mouth twisted ruefully. "They got what was coming to them," Elliot said quietly, making Burl lift his head to meet the sharp, but subtle, glitter in Elliot's eyes.

Eve saw the two men exchange glances she didn't quite understand. She cleared her throat and sipped her coffee before saying, "I fed Elliot some catfish and hush puppies. He seems to think we serve good food."

Burl grinned. "Nothing but the best."

"Elliot has a beautiful hound. Black and tan. His name is Rebel."

"You hunt, boy?"

For the past ten years it had been Elliot's job to hunt

and track, but not four-legged animals, only the two-legged kind. "Once in a while, but I never kill anything. I just let the dog run."

"Guess there's not much hunting to be done around Fort Worth," Burl surmised.

"Not anything that's worth hunting," Elliot told him. He drained the last of his coffee then looked at Eve. "I'd better be going, Eve. It's getting late, and I'm interrupting your father's work."

"Nonsense, Elliot," Burl said. "I never consider Eve's friends an interruption. But if you stay around very long, I'll put you to work."

Elliot smiled faintly and rose to his feet. "I wouldn't mind that at all. In fact, I'd welcome something to do. It gets damn quiet at the house."

"If you can use a hammer and saw, I'd be glad to pay you to work on the new dock."

Elliot held up his hand to Burl's suggestion. "I don't need money. Just something to do."

"Show up anytime. Be glad to have you."

Elliot thanked the older man, then said goodbye. Eve followed him outside to the Jeep.

"I hope Daddy didn't irritate you. He loves me, you see," she said, trying to explain away her father's inquisitive attitude.

Elliot smiled as he swung himself up into the Jeep. Without being told to, Rebel joined him on the opposite seat.

"Your daddy is a good man. I wish I'd had one just like him."

Eve's heart swelled in her breast. "I wish you had, too, Elliot. But I'll share mine with you." She would share a lot of things with him if only he would let her.

She was good through and through, Elliot thought. He didn't want that to change. It was one of the reasons he should stay away from her. But it was too late for that now. Maybe it had been too late from the moment she'd walked into his camp.

"I'll think about that, Eve."

She stepped closer and placed her hand on his arm. It was warm and strong beneath her hand, and the hair felt crisp and tickly to her fingers. She had to curb the urge to cling to him.

"I hope you'll think about me," she said.

His hazel eyes were filled with warmth as they caressed her face. How could he not think about her? "I will. Probably. Sooner or later I'll say to myself, I wonder whatever happened to Eve."

A smile tilted the corner of her lips. "And I'll probably ask myself whatever happened to that difficult man who was living in the woods."

Elliot's eyes rested on her mouth. "You think I'm difficult?"

She let out a jerky breath. "You have your moments."

His response to that was a soft chuckle. Eve went on to say, "I didn't tell Daddy I slept with you."

He gave her a wry smile, liking the way she said "slept with you." "I gathered that much, Eve, when he didn't meet me at the door with a shotgun."

Eve felt herself blushing. "You must think we're terribly old-fashioned."

He shook his head. "I think you've been living in a different world than I."

His words intrigued her. "And which one do you think is better?" she asked.

For an answer he leaned down and kissed her softly on the lips. "I haven't figured that out yet, Eve," he said.

Before she could respond, he started the engine. Eve forced her hand to slide away from his arm. "Goodbye, Elliot," she said, stepping back from the Jeep.

He lifted a hand in farewell, then turned the Jeep around and headed out toward the highway.

Eve walked back to the house with a thoughtful look on her face, and a bit of hope in her heart.

Burl was still drinking his coffee when Eve came through the kitchen door. He looked at his daughter with a mixture of fondness and concern.

"So you like this man, do you?"

Eve nodded and felt herself blushing as she picked up the dirty cups and saucers.

"I like him very much," she confessed, carrying the dishes over to the sink.

Burl sighed, leaned back in his chair and balanced his cup and saucer on his knee. He was a big, strong man. Not just physically, but emotionally, too. Eve had always looked up to him with love and respect, and she'd always valued his opinion, even though she sometimes disagreed with him.

"He's not like anyone you've ever gone around with before," Burl told her.

She met her father's glance. "What do you mean? Don't you like Elliot?"

Burl's straightforward expression didn't alter. "I'd have to say I do like Elliot. He just seems a bit potent for you."

Eve smiled to herself. Her father was right. Elliot was pretty potent. "In other words, you think he's too much man for me?"

Burl shifted in his seat. "Well, I didn't come right out

with that," he said. "I just mean that you've always lived a slow, country life. The men you're used to are far different from Elliot."

"Yes, he is different," Eve agreed. "But not in a bad way."

"No, probably not. I just don't think you're on the same wavelength. I get the idea that he's tough as nails. He didn't get that scar on his lip from practicing his piano lessons."

Eve turned back to the sink and began to wash the dirty cups. "You think he got it fighting."

"I'd bet on it."

"And you think I'm serious about him, don't you?"

Behind her, Burl sighed heavily. "You were giving him looks that I've never seen on your face. That tells me quite a lot, Eve."

Eve kept her eyes on the soapy cup in her hands. Her father knew her so well. "Would that be so bad, if I was serious about him?"

"Maybe, maybe not. I just have the feeling he's a diamond in the rough. You could get hurt if you tried to get inside him."

Eve rinsed the cup and propped it in the drain. "I don't think he wants me, or anyone, to see inside him."

"You don't know anything about him, and he doesn't want to tell you anything. That worries me, Eve."

It bothered Eve, too, because she wanted to know everything about Elliot. She wanted him to share his life, past and present, with her. But she didn't want to force him to do it; she wanted him to willingly open up to her.

Pushing her hair away from her face, she turned to face her father once again. "Elliot is a good man. I know that with all my heart."

Burl leaned forward and placed his empty cup on the table. "I hope so, Evie. I damn well hope so."

To her amazement, Eve saw Elliot the very next afternoon. He was on the roof of the new dock, hammering nails into the corrugated sheet iron that was being used for roofing. He was dressed in jeans and a thick white T-shirt that was already damp with sweat. Two other men were working with him; Bob, their regular worker, and a man Burl had hired from the little town of Hemphill some several miles south of the marina.

None of the men saw Eve approaching, including Elliot, until she called up to him.

"Elliot? Is that you?"

He turned on his haunches and saw her standing on the grassy slope of the water's edge, shading her eyes with her hand.

"Hello, Eve."

"You weren't kidding about working, I see."

He grinned down at her. She made a beautiful picture in a pink printed sundress, with her dark hair tied back into a ponytail with a matching scarf.

"By the way I'm handling this hammer, these guys might think I'm kidding. It's been a long time."

Bob, a hefty man with graying black hair, spoke around a nail in his mouth. "He's doing fine. A born carpenter."

Elliot's grin grew broader. It was good to be around people again, he thought. Regular kind of people who put in an honest day's labor, then went home at night, tired but happy. For a little while, he could almost believe he was just like them.

"That's great," Eve said, feeling very happy at seeing Elliot again, and seeing him making friends with her friends. "I'm afraid I'm not very good with a hammer, so I'd better get back to the kitchen. See you."

Three hours later the roof was completed, and Elliot found Eve in the restaurant kitchen. She was slicing strawberries into a big aluminum bowl wedged between her legs.

"You know," Marcia said, unaware that Elliot had entered the kitchen, "my nephew, Bradley, would love for you to share his apartment over in Natchitoches when you start college. You know, he always did have a crush on you anyway."

Eve grimaced. "That's exactly why it would be impossible to share living quarters with him. In one day's time he'd have me cornered in the bedroom."

Marcia chuckled. "That might not be so bad, Eve. Bradley is kinda cute."

Eve snorted. "Kinda cute and he knows it. Besides—"

Elliot cleared his throat, and both women's heads jerked around in surprise.

"Sorry if I scared you ladies," he said.

Eve jumped to her feet, nearly spilling the strawberries in the process. "Elliot! When did you finish the roof?"

He grinned rather impishly and wiped an arm across his sweaty forehead. "About the time you were being cornered in the bedroom, I'd say."

Eve blushed furiously and glared at Marcia, who laughed.

"Here, let me get you something cool to drink," Eve said to Elliot. "Would you like something to eat, too?" She began to fill a tall glass with ice and tea.

"Actually I was wondering if you'd like to have dinner with me tonight."

"I'd love to," she told him without preamble, then

glanced at Marcia, who was busily pretending not to listen. "Can you make it without me, Mar—"

Before Eve could get the rest out, the older woman winked and said to Elliot, "Take her. Get her out of here and keep her. All night, if you can."

"Marcia!" Eve spluttered.

Elliot chuckled and guided Eve out of the kitchen through the back door exit.

Eve's face was still red once they were outside. Elliot tried to remember when he last saw a woman blush and decided it had been too long.

"She's an impossible matchmaker," Eve told him in an effort to explain Marcia. "She thinks I'm shriveling away, living without a man as I do."

Elliot grinned. "She seems to think I'd be good for you."

Eve laughed, seeing the humor of it all. "Marcia thinks any man would be good for me."

Elliot's brows lifted as he swallowed down the last of his tea. "I don't like that idea."

Eve smiled, liking the possessive sound of his words. "By the time Marcia was my age, she'd been married ten years. She's getting desperate for me."

Elliot tossed the ice from his glass across the green grass, then ran a hand through his dark hair. Eve watched his movements, thinking she loved the way his hair lay sleek and dark against his head.

"And are you? Getting desperate?" he asked.

There was a hint of seriousness in his voice that Eve couldn't quite ignore. "For what?"

He gave a negligible shrug and said, "A man. Marriage."

"That's Marcia's idea. Not mine." But she was, she

thought, a little bit desperate for him. It was a new and scary feeling for Eve. She wondered what he would think if he knew. Maybe he did know, and his question was his way of telling her that he did.

"Are you?" she put to him. "Desperate for a woman?"

He chuckled lowly. "If I hang around you long enough, Eve, I just might be."

The afternoon sun was hot, and the humidity hung in the sky like a dirty haze. Elliot felt the heat and realized they were standing in the broiling hot sun as if neither one of them had good sense.

"Are we going to dinner, or not?" he asked.

"I thought we were. Where are we going, Elliot?"

Guiding her toward the bungalow, he said, "Anywhere you choose. As long as you let me stop by my house so that I can change out of these sweaty clothes."

While Elliot waited, Eve hurriedly changed into a deep blue sheath with narrow straps that crisscrossed over her bare back.

After writing her father a note telling him where she'd gone, they left in Elliot's Jeep.

Driving over the dirt road to his place, Elliot's eyes kept straying to Eve. The blue dress she was wearing invited him to look at her softly rounded curves. She'd brushed her hair loose against her shoulders, and the wind rushing through the Jeep had whipped it into a web of dark curls around her face. He decided it was like a bit of heaven to have her next to him like this.

"It was a very nice thing of you to do, coming over and helping finish the roof," she told him. "Daddy will really appreciate it."

"I didn't do it to impress your father, or you either, as far as that goes."

Sighing, she frowned at him. Did he always read things the wrong way? "I didn't think you did it to impress anyone," she said in a wounded voice.

He shook his head as he shifted the Jeep down before turning into the driveway. "Sorry, Eve. I—it's been a long time since—Well, neighbor helping neighbor just didn't happen where I lived. Not unless you wanted to be accused of having ulterior motives. I guess I'm just not used to receiving thank-yous."

Her face softened as she studied his profile. He was so tough-looking on the outside, but underneath all that steel were soft little places that could be touched.

"I don't ever think of anyone having ulterior motives."

"Maybe you should," Elliot said. "It might keep you out of trouble."

He killed the motor and looked over at her. Eve suddenly remembered the night in the woods when he'd warned her about trusting people. She could still recall the feel of his strong fingers against her throat.

Eve said, "I don't need to think about such awful things. Not with my friends. Not with you."

She trusted him. And that did strange things to Elliot's heart. He looked away from her, then slid lithely to the ground.

Looking through the door at her, he said, "You still think I'm that honest man you slept with on the lake."

Eve climbed out of her side of the Jeep. They walked to the front gate before either of them spoke again.

"I know that you are," Eve said with conviction as they stood close together.

Elliot looked at her, knowing he desperately wanted to kiss her there in the fading light, the sultry heat pressing in on them.

Yet her gray eyes looked at him tenderly, full of trust and caring. It made Elliot feel guilty, and more than a bit frustrated. Being with Eve was teaching him things about women that he hadn't even known.

"Come on," he told her, shoving open the rickety wooden gate. "I'd better hurry and change or we'll never get to eat."

Eve followed him through the yard. She noticed he'd mowed the lawn and cleared away some of the black-berry brambles. It made the place appear a bit homier, yet it somehow reminded Eve how alone Elliot was out here in the woods.

Elliot unlocked the front door. As they went inside, Eve said, "I can see you're from the city."

"What gave it away? My lack of chewing tobacco?" he asked dryly.

"You're being tacky now, Elliot. I was merely refer-ring to your locking the door in the daytime."

He looked at her impatiently; yet even so, Eve caught the glimmer of amusement in his eyes.

"I suppose if you were me, you wouldn't lock it. You'd trust every Tom, Dick and Harry that came by."

She smiled and ran her hands down the sides of her hips. Elliot's eyes followed her movements along the close-fitting dress. He wondered if his grandpa's old four-poster could stand the strain if he were to carry Eve in there now and make passionate love to her.

Thinking the bed could probably stand it, but not his peace of mind, he let out a long breath and looked away from her.

"Only people with something to hide lock their doors," she told him while taking a seat on an old, but clean, couch. "have you ever thought about that?"

For one second Eve thought his expression turned cold. But then it was gone so quickly that she wondered if she'd imagined it.

"I thought we might drive up to Longview," he said, changing the subject completely. "Is that all right with you?"

Eve nodded. "I'd like that. It's been a long time since I've been up that way."

"I won't be long," he said. "But you might find it cooler if you sat out on the back porch." His hand reached to the hem of his T-shirt and with one sudden twist he pulled it over his head. He turned to start down the hall toward the bathroom, but something on Eve's face made him go still.

She stared at his naked chest. He was all lean muscle, and the skin was just as dark as that on his face. Black hair matted across his chest then arrowed down toward his navel. Her mind swam with the idea of touching him there.

As their eyes met, something tightened inside her. It gave Eve a strange, reckless feeling that she had not known before.

Without speaking, she rose from her seat and walked over to him. She didn't understand why she felt so at one with him. She had felt that way from the very beginning. Now it did not seem strange at all to put her hands on his bare shoulders.

"Will you kiss me, Elliot?"

Chapter Six

As soon as Eve's hands touched Elliot, his insides went a little wild. It was a struggle for him not to pick her up and carry her to the bedroom. He wanted to forget about the rightness or wrongness, and what might be good for either of them.

"You're flirting with starvation, lady," he said huskily, but already his mouth was headed for hers.

Eve moaned as his lips took hers, softly, sweetly. She slid her hands up and down his chest, loving the heavy feel of his muscles flexing beneath the pressure of her fingers. His skin was satiny and damp with sweat. She knew it would be an exquisite feeling to brush her bare breasts against him. And it shocked Eve somewhat to know that if he would only ask, she would peel her dress away and let him make love to her.

Her hands slipped up over his shoulders and around

his neck. Elliot felt his control weaken when her soft curves nestled up against him. His fingers were on her back, pressing her hips into him. He wanted her with a vengeance. Not just her body, but also her love.

The thought came out of nowhere and knocked him for a loop. He pulled away from her abruptly, his breaths coming quick and hot. He looked at her face, and his heart contracted at the drowsy desire in her gray eyes.

He was falling in love with this sweet, beautiful country girl, and he suddenly knew he was in a hell of a mess.

"I'd better go change, Eve," he whispered, pulling her arms from around his neck.

"Elliot—if you—"

Seeing the confused look on her face, he smoothed his hand over her cheek, saying, "I won't be long, Eve."

She felt her insides melt with love and longing as she watched him disappear into the bathroom. She suddenly remembered what Marcia had told her about knowing when you'd found the right man. Eve now knew that the right man for her was Elliot. She knew it every time she touched him, looked at him, thought of him.

The sound of the shower running interrupted her thoughts. She leaned down and picked up Elliot's T-shirt from where he'd dropped it on the floor.

Wondering where he kept his dirty clothes, she walked out to the kitchen, noticing on the way that the old house was still in surprisingly good shape. Wallpaper covered most of the walls, and a brick fireplace was built back to back in the living room and kitchen. Eve supposed the Marshalls had once heated the place with wood.

She wondered if Elliot had ideas of staying in east Texas, living here in this old house and raising a family.

She wondered, also, if any of that could include her and her plans for law school.

She found a basket sitting on top of a washing machine at the back of the kitchen. She'd just tossed his T-shirt into it when she heard him call her name.

"Eve?"

Walking back to the living room, she peered down the hallway to see his head sticking around the bathroom door. She looked at him questioningly, and he smiled at her.

"Would you mind getting me a beer from the refrigerator? Get yourself something, too, if you like."

"Sure," she said. "Just give me a minute."

Back in the kitchen, she opened the refrigerator and rummaged past a plate of leftover fried chicken and a bowl of mashed potatoes covered with thick white gravy. Eve grimaced at the sight of the gravy. Everyone knew milk gravy just wasn't any good warmed over, and she hated to think of Elliot eating it. She hoped he was saving that dish for Rebel.

Eve pulled out a bottle of beer and a can of soda for herself. The beer had a flat metal lid that was supposed to twist off by hand. When Eve tried it, she couldn't budge it. Setting the can of soda aside, she grasped the bottle with both hands and twisted harder. The cap wouldn't move a fraction. Quickly she began to look for a bottle opener.

The pistol was in the end drawer, next to the wall. At first, Eve merely gave it a cursory glance. It wasn't a surprise to find that Elliot owned a gun. Most everyone she knew owned guns. They just naturally went along with hunting and country living. Yet after a longer, second glance, Eve decided there was something different about this pistol.

A strange premonition suddenly chilled her. Her eyes still on the open drawer, she absently placed the beer bottle on the cabinet counter. Then, taking a deep breath, she reached out warily and touched the worn leather holster.

It was not one that was worn at the hip, but a shoulder holster that was normally used by federal agents or plainclothes policemen.

Her heart beating faster, Eve started to pick it up, then suddenly halted. At the back of the drawer was a flat leather case the same color as the gun holster.

Eve didn't question what she was about to do. She only knew that something was compelling her to know more about the man who had captured her heart.

The shiny, oval badge opened in her palm. Eve stared at it, finding the authority connected with the object a bit formidable.

Slowly her eyes began to take in the information. Across from the badge was an identification card with Elliot's picture on it. Lieutenant Joe Elliot, she read. Fort Worth Police Department. Height: Six feet. Weight: One hundred-seventy-five pounds. She scanned on down the physical identification, but it barely registered in Eve's shocked mind.

Elliot was a policeman! At least this said he was. So what was he doing in rural east Texas? Was he still a policeman, or had he quit the force? Her mind whirled with the information she'd just discovered.

Footsteps echoed on the linoleum, then Elliot's voice sounded behind her. "Did you find the beer?"

The badge still in her hand, Eve turned slowly, lifted her head and looked at him. Her wide eyes mirrored the shock she felt over her discovery.

"Your name is Elliot," she said rather inanely.

He was stuffing the tails of a blue-and-white-striped shirt into his blue jeans. He finished the task, zipping the fly and buttoning the waist of his jeans before answering. "I know. That *is* what you call me," he said.

She sputtered with frustration. "I know—but I thought—your last name was Marshall, like your grandparents.

Elliot shook his head, moved to the cabinet and picked up the beer Eve had forgotten. She watched him twist off the cap in one effortless motion.

Without looking at her, he said, "Marshall was my mother's maiden name."

While Eve tried to digest this information, he tilted his head back and downed about a third of the cold beer.

"Does anyone call you Joe?"

A faint smirk marred his face. "Not many people care that I have a first name."

She wondered what he meant by that, but there was a more pressing question already on her tongue. "You've been here on the lake for seven months, you said. Did you resign from the police force or something?"

He gave a brief shake of his head. "I've taken an indefinite leave of absence. I haven't resigned—not yet."

"Not yet?" she echoed, totally amazed at his indifference. "Then you're thinking about resigning?"

After a couple more drinks of beer he said impatiently, "Yes. I am. Now, are we going to go eat, or not?"

Stung by his attitude, Eve could merely stare at him. He was putting her in her place, telling her that his life was none of her business. If he had struck her physically, it couldn't have hurt more.

Swallowing down the sudden lump in her throat, she placed the badge back in the drawer, then pushed it shut.

"Yes. I'm ready," she said quietly without looking at him. "I'd like to go now."

Quickly she walked around him and into the living room. She was picking up her purse from the couch when his footsteps sounded behind her. She felt her body tense at his approach.

"Eve?"

She couldn't bring herself to look at him. It hurt too much, and she'd hate to cry in front of him.

"Yes."

"I didn't—" Elliot stopped, not knowing how to go on as he studied the back of her bent head. He knew he'd hurt her, and that was exactly what he was trying to avoid. Still, how could he explain something to her that he'd spent the past seven months trying to forget?

He let out a deep breath and tried again. "I'm sorry I was so short with you."

Eve suddenly felt weak and shaky, and she turned to him, catching his eyes with hers. "It's all right, Elliot," she whispered hoarsely. "I have no right to question you about your life. It's your own business whether you're a cop or in some other profession."

Elliot felt something twisting and tearing inside of him. "It's not that I—it's just something I don't like to talk about," he finally managed to get out.

Eve heard the struggle in his voice, and she suddenly knew that something had gone terribly wrong in Elliot's life. Maybe it was still wrong. She wanted to know, but she would never try to force it out of him. She wanted him close to her, close enough to want to tell her everything.

Her heart was full of love and concern as she stepped toward him. "It's all right, Elliot. Really."

His dark eyes flicked over her, and Eve watched as the anguish slowly slipped from his face. He reached for her hands, then, moaning softly, he pulled her into his arms.

"Hell, Eve," he murmured into her hair. "I don't even know how to talk with anyone anymore. I don't know how to be with anyone—with you. I can't share myself—and—"

Eve's head twisted a protest against his hard chest. "Don't say that, Elliot. You can talk to me—be with me."

She felt his chest rise on a deep breath, and then his forefinger was on her chin, lifting her face up to his.

His expression was intense as he said, "Yes, you're the only one I can be with. And I guess a part of me never wanted you to know that I was a cop."

Amazed at his words, Eve hungrily searched his face for answers. "Why?" she whispered.

He shrugged, and his hand lifted and stroked her dark hair gently, lovingly.

One corner of his mouth curled wryly. "Cops are bad risks, you know. There's a lot of people out there who like us better dead than alive."

She shuddered at his cold observation. "You make it sound like a war," she told him.

He smiled with faint mockery. "I suppose it is. Not just with the criminals, but with the long, exhausting hours, the total dedication you have to give. It doesn't leave much time for anything else in your life."

"Is that why you're thinking about quitting?"

He looked into her eyes for long minutes. Eve looked

back and watched dark, troubled shadows cross his face. Finally he gave one brief shake of his head. "No." He sighed. "That isn't the reason."

"You don't have to tell me, you know," she said softly.

One hand drifted down to her face, and Eve felt herself melting as his fingertips traced a gentle pattern upon her cheek.

"Things went wrong for me, Eve. I don't know where or why. But something happened, and when it was all over I came out of it wondering what the hell our legal system was all about. I spent ten years on the force, and all that time I thought I was making a difference. Now I know that kind of thinking was a pile of rotten garbage. And why should I want to go back to a pile of rotten garbage? If you don't believe in what you're doing, you might as well throw in the towel."

Eve's heart ached for him. "Ten years is a long time. I wouldn't have to ask anyone to know that you're a good cop."

He dropped his hold on her and savagely raked both hands through the sides of his hair. "You wouldn't say that, Eve, if you knew all the details. And frankly, I don't want you to know them. Not right now, anyway. Do you hate me for that, honey? Because I can't tell you?"

Eve's fingers curled into the hard muscles of his chest. Her eyes filled with trust and understanding as she looked up at him. "I could never hate you for anything, Elliot. I know that you're a good, honest man. And I know that whatever happened, if things went bad, it wasn't because of any wrongdoing on your part."

He felt himself tremble with relief, and he had to acknowledge to himself that he'd been afraid. Joe Elliot, a man who'd never been afraid of anything in his life, had been afraid that Eve would turn away from him. But here she was trusting him blindly, unquestioningly. He felt better than he had in a long, long time.

Eve watched a broad smile spread across his mouth and her heart lifted. She smiled back at him.

"You're precious, Eve," he said.

She shook her head, her cheeks turning pink at his compliment. "Not really," she told him, then reached up and caressed his face with her fingers.

"Why don't you let me cook dinner for you here, instead of going out?"

Surprised, he lifted his brows. "I wanted to treat you tonight."

She laughed and pulled away from him. Then, gathering his hand in hers, she pulled him toward the kitchen. "It will be a treat to cook for you. Come on, show me what you want."

"I don't have many groceries," he warned.

"That doesn't matter. We'll find something. Do you like biscuits?"

He chuckled softly, suddenly liking the idea of having her here, alone with him, instead of in a restaurant. "I love biscuits, Eve."

"Good," she said, already reaching to open the cabinets. Taking down a sack of flour, she said, "I'll mix them while you choose what you want with them."

He started toward the refrigerator, then suddenly turned and snapped his fingers with sudden dawning. "I know something," he said.

Reaching for Eve's hand he pulled her toward the back screen door.

"What is it? Do you have a garden back here?" she asked.

"No. No garden. I don't know anything about growing vegetables." He led her across the porch and down the steps. Rebel, who was lying under a shade tree, lifted his head and watched as Elliot tugged Eve over to an old smokehouse.

"Really, Elliot, don't tell me you've tried to cure a hog in this heat!" she said, thinking it would be the only reason for something edible to be in a smokehouse.

Instead of opening the door, Elliot squatted down on his haunches and began to search for something beneath the old building. "Not a hog, honey."

He pulled out an oblong container filled with muddy water. Eve looked at him in amazement. "That's going to be our supper?"

He smiled smugly. "Look closer. My game ranger friend, Caleb, brought them by yesterday. He thought I might want to use them for fish bait."

"Crawdads," Eve guessed, kneeling down next to him to take a closer look.

By now Rebel had joined them. He licked Eve on the arm, then sniffed at the muddy water.

Two pincers and a pair of black whiskers suddenly rose menacingly up out of the water. Rebel barked and Eve laughed.

"They might be scary now, Rebel, but they'll taste good later on," she told the dog.

Elliot chuckled, then asked Eve, "You know how to cook crawdads?"

She gave him a sexy, know-it-all look. "Could I

live in Cajun country all my life and not know how to boil crawdads?"

His response was a laugh that made Eve feel warm and good. It was wonderful to be with him, and the night loomed ahead of her, long and promising.

Eve showed Elliot everything about boiling crawdads. After he'd cleaned them with fresh water, she put a big pot on the stove and filled it with water and spices, including a hefty amount of cayenne pepper.

"Don't ever cook a dead crawdad," she told him once the water started to boil.

"How do you tell if they're dead or just playing possum?"

Eve grinned at his question as he stood beside her, a galvanized water bucket in her hand. The little creatures made scratching and squeaking noises against the metal as they tried to climb the sides of the dry bucket.

"A straight tail," she told him. "It will give 'em away every time."

He laughed, and she could tell from the sparkle in his eye that he was considering making a crude comment.

"You can forget about the joke," she told him with a laugh. "The water is ready. Do you want to pour them in? Or would you rather I do it?"

"I've been told I'm heartless. So maybe I'd better send the little things to their death," he told her.

"Here," she said, holding out a quilted glove. "Put this on or you might get pinched."

Elliot put the glove on, then raked in the crawdads while Eve stirred them into the boiling water.

"How do you tell when they're done?" he asked.

"Easy," Eve said. "They'll float."

He sidled closer to her. Eve looked up at him as he

touched her hair. A lazy smile curved his mouth. "I like having you here like this, Eve. No one has ever cooked for me before."

Her eyebrows went up in a disbelieving way, and he went on, "I mean, someone like you. My mother always had to work at a job to make a living for us. She never had much time for cooking. And later—the women—" He broke off, a sheepish look covering his face. "Well, maybe you don't want to hear—"

Her smile turned a bit wry. He didn't have to tell Eve what type of women he meant. Elliot was a sexy man. She doubted he'd ever lacked feminine attention. "That the girlfriends in your past weren't the kitchen types," she finished tactfully, and turned her eyes back on the boiling pot.

Elliot watched her face turn a pretty pink and smiled at the delicate way she'd completed his sentence. Her obvious innocence was something new to Elliot. He'd always believed that he preferred experienced women, but Eve was quickly changing that idea.

"Well, er, no, not exactly."

Eve hated the idea of his making love to another woman, and the feeling amazed her because she'd never been a jealous or possessive person before now. Particularly where boyfriends were concerned. She supposed that was because she'd never been that serious about any of them before—until now.

She watched the crawdads begin to rise to the top of the boiling pot and wondered why it had been so easy to become serious about Elliot. "So. Are you learning anything from me—about the kitchen, I mean?"

He shrugged and grinned. "About cooking crawdads. Not about women."

Eve pursed her lips. "I have the feeling that you've never really wanted to know that much about women. I doubt you've ever really wanted one in your life for more than twenty-four hours at a time."

Elliot chuckled, and Eve decided there was a cocky sound to it. She gave him a sidelong glance, then felt herself growing warm as his hazel eyes caught and held hers.

"Maybe that's because I never had twenty-four hours free until I left Fort Worth," he admitted.

His words told Eve two things. That he'd worked too much, and that if he'd had a woman in his life, he hadn't spent much time with her. Not the kind of time a lasting relationship would require.

He must have tried living as a man unto himself, she thought. Not wanting or needing anyone else. It was difficult for Eve to imagine herself being that set apart, that alone.

"And what about now?" she asked huskily. "You have lots of time on your hands."

Elliot's mouth slanted to a sexy, suggestive grin. "That's right. I have plenty of twenty-four hours." His knuckles brushed up and down her bare arm. "And you are a woman," he needlessly reminded her.

Drawing in a shaky breath, she met his eyes and smiled. "And right now the crawdads are floating."

Elliot peered lazily over the edge of the pot. "So they are," he drawled. "I guess we'd better eat."

It was unusually warm, even for a May night in Texas. Elliot placed an oscillating fan on the cabinet counter to stir the air while they ate.

The crawdads were hot and spicy, and the biscuits light and flaky. Elliot stuffed himself and complimented

Eve on her cooking so many times that she finally told him to hush.

After they finished their meal, the two of them carried their coffee to the steps of the back porch. It was dark now, but the sky was clear and a big yellow moon was beginning to rise over the edge of the treetops.

The cooler night air had finally begun to move in, and Eve breathed in deeply, appreciating the beauty of the evening.

"So, when do you plan to start college?" Elliot asked.

Eve looked over at him. They were sitting side by side on the top step, their shoulders almost touching. She loved being close to him, and wondered if he felt the same about her.

"This fall," she answered. "Actually I feel sort of guilty about it. I've always helped daddy with the marina. I don't feel completely right about leaving it all with him."

He sipped his coffee, trying to imagine what it would be like with her gone. He knew he would miss her like hell. "I wouldn't look at it that way. You should have your opportunity to spread your wings. I'm sure your daddy sees it that way, too."

She set her empty cup down on the step below him. "Of course he doesn't expect me to always stay at the marina. But as you heard the other night, he's not all that keen on my going to law school."

Eve could feel his eyes upon her, and she turned to look at him once more.

"I expect that's because he doesn't want you hurt, Eve. He knows that once you get into law you'll be faced with ugly, hideous things. It's not something I'd want for a daughter of mine."

She thought about his words, wondering if he'd think

the same way about a wife. But then she had to bring herself up short. Elliot was a loner. He was far from the marrying kind. He had that love 'em and leave 'em look stamped all over him.

"I've considered all that, Elliot. And I know that I won't be dealing with pretty things. But that's part of the challenge, I think. Besides, you and Daddy are way ahead of things. It takes years to get a law degree, and even then I couldn't get appointed to an assistant district attorney's position without first gaining lots of experience. It'll be years before any of that happens."

Thank God, Elliot said to himself.

"I'll be old and crusty by then," she went on in a teasing tone. "Tough and cranky, too, probably. I'll be able to handle anything."

Elliot didn't find her words amusing. Eve would never be tough and crusty. Sharp and intelligent, but never tough-skinned. After a while she'd be hurt and disillusioned, and her spark for living would eventually be extinguished. It had happened to him, and he didn't want it to happen to her.

"Don't count on it, Eve. Law is ugly, any way you look at it."

She pursed her lips at his cynical observation. "So why did you get into it, then?"

He frowned and tossed away the last sip of his coffee. "Because I was like you once, all full of fire and determination to go out and conquer the bad guys. I thought I'd be doing something meaningful with my life. Hell, wasn't that a joke," he muttered.

"I'm not laughing," she said.

He looked at her as if he wanted to say more. Eve wondered what kind of demons he'd lived with these past months. What ever they were, it was obvious they were still inside him.

Suddenly he reached for her hand and tugged her up from the step.

"Come on," he said huskily. "Let's walk."

He led her across the yard and out a back gate that was even more rickety than the front one. They followed a well-worn path that led into the woods.

"It's quiet and lovely here," Eve observed as they strolled beneath towering loblolly pines. Frogs and crickets sang out from nearby underbrush. Eve loved the peacefulness of country living. She wondered if Elliot had found the quietness soothing or irritating after living in a big city. "Did the slowness of this life bother you when you first came back?"

The only light was that of the moon filtering through the boughs of the pines. Eve could barely make out the grimace on his face.

"At first it didn't matter. All I did was sit and brood, anyway."

"That sounds very productive," she said mockingly.

His hand was on her arm, and Eve felt his fingers tighten just a fraction.

"What else is a man supposed to do when he's mad?"

Eve took a deep breath. "You could have tried fighting back," she suggested.

"I tried that for ten years. I decided I was tired of fighting a useless battle."

Moments passed as they continued to walk over the path that was softly carpeted with fallen pine needles.

"Sounds like you were a burnt-out cop," Eve finally replied in a thoughtful voice. "That you hated your job and that it was time for you to get out of it anyway."

Jolted by her words, Elliot growled, "I wasn't that way at all!" Then added more gently, "I admit that I put in too many hours, but—I wasn't burnt-out."

"Then you liked being a cop?"

Her question made him uncomfortable because it made him face things he just wasn't ready to face. "Yeah," he said with a sigh. "I did like being a cop."

"But now you think you don't like it," she said.

"Eve," he said impatiently, "why do you always put things in such simple terms? You can't just like, or not like, something."

Eve chuckled as a spurt of encouragement filled her. She was beginning to see underneath Elliot's frustrated attitude. He wasn't completely indifferent to his job or the past devotion he'd given his career in law enforcement.

"Yes, you can, Elliot. I like hamburgers. I don't like hot dogs. Very simple."

"You're maddening," he said, but there was a teasing note in his voice.

They topped a rise, and Eve made a small sound of pleasure. Below them was a fairly large pond with a long wooden dock built out over the water at one end.

"Did you build the dock?" she asked.

"It's been here for years. My grandfather built it. I did some repair work on it a couple of weeks ago."

Eve jogged eagerly ahead of him and onto the dock. The water was still, and appeared as mirrored glass beneath the moonlight. At the far end lily pads grew in clusters at the water's edge.

"Can you swim here?" she asked, her eyes drinking in the beautiful setting.

"It's better than a pool," Elliot said, coming up behind her. "No chemicals, and the bottom is clean and gravelly. It's not over your head anywhere, except on the far end down by the lily pads. Maybe I'll invite you over for a swim," he suggested in a warm, indulgent voice.

"I'd be put out if you didn't," she assured him, taking a seat at the edge of the wooden platform.

She looked up as Elliot sat down close behind her. "This is one of my favorite places," he told her, leaning lazily back on one elbow. "My grandfather would bring me down here, and we'd throw biscuit crumbs into the pond and watch the sun perch feed. Lord, was that ever a long time ago."

"Did you ever fish for them?"

Elliot shook his head. "He never was much on fishing. He was a hunter. I guess I took after him, because I ended up being a hunter of sorts. A detective in vice has to do lots of hunting, trapping and tracking."

So he'd worked in vice, she thought. Nasty business. She could only think of one thing worse, and that was homicide.

"Did your grandfather urge you to become a policeman?"

He shook his head. "He urged me to do whatever I thought would make me the happiest. God, I hope he can't see me now. He used to be so proud of me—but now—"

He didn't finish, and from the raw sound of his voice she knew he couldn't bear to say how he felt. With all her heart, Eve wanted to comfort him. Leaning closer, she covered his big hand with her much smaller one.

"He'd still be proud of you. Everyone has their down times. You'll come out of all this even better than you were."

Elliot shifted toward her. Eve felt herself glow with heat as his hand lifted to touch her face.

"I'd like to believe that, Eve. And I can almost believe it when I look at you."

Eve's heart began to thud. He was so close that the scent of him surrounded her, the warmth of him reached out to her. She'd never thought about touching a man the way she did Elliot. He was in her heart, just as surely as the stars shone over their heads.

She leaned over and placed her palms against his chest. "You should believe it, Elliot."

Wordlessly he meshed his fingers in her hair and drew her face to his. He touched her lips softly, coaxing and urging Eve to take what she wanted from him.

She responded hungrily, taking pleasure in nibbling at his lower lip. Desire washed through Elliot like an ocean wave. He deepened the kiss, drawing on her sweetness with undisguised hunger.

Eve opened her mouth for his searching tongue, then felt her senses reeling under its intimate exploration. Intuitively her body flattened against his, and she pushed her fingers into his dark hair.

Elliot groaned and hugged her tighter against him. In the process, Eve's dress rode up above her knees. Elliot took advantage of the fact and rubbed his tough palms up and down her bare thighs. The caresses sent shivers of delight over Eve's skin.

"I feel so close to you, Elliot," she whispered once he'd released her mouth from the bondage of his kiss. "I have from the very beginning."

Elliot felt his heart turn over, then swell inexplicably in his chest.

"I feel close to you, Eve. Closer than I've ever been to anyone."

Suddenly tears burned behind her eyes. She loved this man so much. Surely he must feel it every time she touched him, every time she looked at him. Her hands slid to his face, and one finger traced the scar on his lip.

Elliot trembled beneath her caress. He'd been touched by many women in the past, but he'd never been touched with love. He now knew the difference.

"I know that you don't want to be serious about me," she said softly, looking down at his face and letting her eyes slide adoringly over its moon-washed angles.

Elliot looked up at her, his face solemn, his eyes searching. "I thought I was serious about someone once. But when things went bad for me, she deserted me like a rat on a sinking ship."

Eve's heart twisted painfully at his admission. "Did you love her?"

His head moved back and forth. "I didn't know what love was, and I seriously doubt she did, either. If she had, she wouldn't have left me."

"You don't think I'd be like her, do you? Because I wouldn't be, Elliot. I could never leave you—"

"Eve," he breathed, shaken by her unexpected vow. Elliot had believed that over the past few months he'd grown too cynical, too hard-nosed to be touched by anyone or anything, particularly a woman. But Eve was proving how wrong he'd been.

He felt the warmth of her breath and the gentleness in her fingers. And on her face was a love and tenderness that he'd never been shown before. He didn't want to lose that. He didn't want to lose her.

"I've lost a lot of things, Eve. And I've survived, but

if you—if you left me, I don't know if I'd want to survive."

Eve drew in a small gasp of surprise. She opened her mouth, but Elliot went on before she had the chance to speak.

"You think I don't want to be serious about you. And maybe I didn't at first. I sure as hell tried not to be— but I am. You've become the most important thing in my life, and I need for you to know that."

Eve thought her heart would burst with joy. "I love you, Elliot. You may not want to hear that. But—"

"Oh yes, Eve. Say it again, honey. Let me hear it again," he whispered.

Happy tears stung her eyes as she looked into his and repeated the words with even greater fervor, "I love you, Joe Elliot. I love you."

Chapter Seven

"Elliot is a policeman, Daddy."

Burl looked up from his morning paper as Eve set a plate of bacon and eggs in front of him.

"What did you say?"

She met her father's gaze. "I said Elliot is a policeman."

Burl shook his head back and forth in a slow, disbelieving way. "That's a hell of a thing to spring on me this early in the morning!" He reached for the salt and pepper shakers.

Eve shrugged one shoulder. Her father's reaction was just as she'd expected. "I thought it was something you'd want to know," she told him.

This brought Burl's head up again. "Why?" he asked, then gave his daughter a long, measured look. "Are you trying to tell me you're thinking about marrying this man?"

"I'm thinking about it. I don't know if Elliot has thought in those terms—yet."

Burl sighed expressively. He flattened both palms against the tabletop, and his usually ruddy complexion paled beneath the kitchen light. Eve knew she'd floored her father.

"You say Elliot's a policeman, then what's he doing living here? Back in the woods?"

Eve dropped her eyes from his. "He's on an indefinite leave of absence. Something happened back in Forth Worth, and he—he's considering quitting the force," she said.

"Did he tell you what happened?"

She shook her head. "Not exactly. But he will."

Burl snorted and began to chop his egg into a pile of mush. "You're asking to be hurt, Evie. You don't know this man. For God's sake, you've only just met him a few weeks ago."

"That's long enough," she told her father.

"You don't know what the man's been mixed up in. Things go on in those big cities, Eve, that country folks like us can't even imagine. Cops go bad. For all you know he was kicked off the force—"

Eve was suddenly angry at her father for wanting to believe the worst of Elliot.

"No, that's not true," she argued. "I don't even know why you would think such a thing!"

"Do you know for certain that he hasn't been kicked out? It looks pretty damn suspicious with him living like a recluse out there in that old house—"

Angry and disappointed, Eve turned away from Burl and headed back to the sink of dirty dishes.

"Yes, I do know, Daddy," she said sharply. "He

still has his badge and gun. He's a lieutenant, a detective in vice."

Eve didn't turn to see his reaction, but she could hear his heavy sigh of resignation. After a moment he said, "I'm sorry, darlin'. I guess—you're my little girl, honey. I want good things for you. That's not hard to understand, is it?"

"I understand your motives. I'm just disappointed that you're so quick to judge him. If anything, I thought you had more faith in me."

"Aw, honey, it's not that I have anything against Elliot. I just never expected you to be attracted to a man like him. But if you say he's a good man, then more than likely he is. I just hope to goodness you think this thing through, Evie."

Eve could have told her father that thinking about Elliot and her future was just about the only thing she'd done this past month since she'd met him.

"He cares about me, I know he does," she told her father.

Burl didn't argue with Eve on that point. "So, what's going to happen if he goes back to being a policeman?"

"I'm hoping he'll ask me to go with him," she confessed.

"You think you could handle something like that?" Burl asked. "The danger, the odd hours?"

"For Elliot—yes, I'm sure of it." What she wasn't sure of was Elliot. His life was hanging in limbo, and that left her hanging, too.

"Well, I could almost be happy about that if it would make you forget this lawyer business."

Eve turned around, shaking her head as she did. "I'm not forgetting that, either. Elliot's been in law for the past ten years. He understands how I feel."

Burl pursed his lips as he reached for his coffee cup. "But he doesn't like it."

Eve flushed. "That's just because he's soured right now."

"Evie, in the past three years two men have asked to marry you and you turned down both of them. And either man could have given you a secure future. Now here you are wanting to give your heart to a man who lives on the edge. I'll never understand women," he muttered as an afterthought.

A faint smile crossed Eve's face. "You always did say I was like Mama, and you said you two fell in love within two days. And you only had ten dollars in your pocket at the time," she reminded him.

Knowing he couldn't argue with that, Burl threw up his hands and laughed. "You're like your mother all right," he agreed, then in a more serious tone he added, "If Elliot is the man you want, Evie, then I won't stand in your way. But just make sure, honey girl. Just make sure."

Later that afternoon, after Eve had finished her work, she jammed her swimsuit and cover-up in a tote bag and climbed into her pickup.

The day was hot and muggy with a few thunderclouds hanging overhead. Eve was feeling the heat as her pickup jostled slowly over the dirt road leading to Elliot's house.

The night before, when he'd taken her home, he'd invited her to come over for a swim today. She was sure the invitation had been an excuse to spend time with her, and that idea made her happy. Still, she was beginning to wonder where all this was leading.

Elliot said her cared about her; he didn't want to lose her. But even so, how could he plan any kind of future when he didn't even know what he wanted out of life?

Right now he seemed to want her, but in the end, Eve knew that would not be enough. It was always a mistake to think you could be happy living your life solely for another person. You had to be happy with yourself first. And she knew that Elliot was a long step from that.

When Eve arrived at Elliot's there was a Louisiana State pickup parked in front. She could hear its two-way radio crackling intermittently as she walked up to the gate.

Elliot was sitting on the porch, and another man, close to his own age, sat relaxed on the top step. He was wearing a gray cowboy hat and an official khaki shirt over a pair of blue jeans. he was blond and rather good-looking, and he smiled with interest as Eve pushed through the wooden gate and entered the yard.

Elliot was sitting on the floor of the porch, his shoulders propped lazily against one of the wooden posts. Rebel was sitting at his side, snapping at a fly that was pestering his long ears.

Eve caught Elliot's eyes and felt the good, warm feeling that she experienced every time she looked at him.

"Hello, Elliot. Have I come at a bad time?"

The man spoke quickly. "I'd say you've come at a perfect time. Hello, I'm Caleb Jones," he said with great enthusiasm while extending his hand to Eve.

She reached out to shake it, and her eye caught sight of the badge pinned to his shirt pocket. "Nice to meet you. My name is Eve Crawford."

"So it is," he said, holding her hand with pointed enjoyment. "My pleasure, Miss Eve."

"Caleb has a nasty reputation with women, Eve. You'll probably have to slap him to get your hand back," Elliot spoke up in a dry voice.

Caleb chuckled good-naturedly and released Eve's hand. She walked over and sat down close to Elliot.

Without saying anything he put his arm around her shoulder, and Eve smiled warmly up at him.

The blond man grimaced with exaggeration. "Oh, so that's how it is."

Elliot gave him a smug smile. "Texas girls have more sense than to look at a Louisiana man."

"Texas girls come over to our side when they discover their men are all brag and no brains."

Eve smiled to herself. Obviously Elliot knew Caleb Jones very well.

"You live in Louisiana, Mr. Jones?" Eve asked

"Honey, don't call him Mr. Jones. You'll give him a complex," Elliot told her.

Caleb ignored Elliot's barbed remark and smiled at Eve. "That's right, Miss Eve, near Natchitoches, as a matter of fact."

"Oh, really. I'll be starting college there this fall," she replicd.

Caleb's smile broadened. "Well now, that's the nicest news I've heard in a long time. Old Elliot will be back in Fort Worth by then, and—"

"Old Elliot is about to bust Mr. Jones in the mouth," Elliot warned in a low growl.

Caleb laughed, obviously getting a kick out of raising Elliot's hackles. "Well, I'd better be moseying back my way. Elliot, I don't suppose you'd want to do some more babysitting for me?"

Without thinking, Eve asked, "You have children?"

He laughed. "Gators, Miss Eve. They're like babies. Precious, you know. Sometimes people come down here thinking they can turn my babies into a purse or a pair of shoes. And me being a game ranger, I just don't take kindly to that."

"I'm sure you wouldn't," Eve said, realizing this was Elliot's game ranger friend he'd first mentioned to her that night in the woods.

"Have you had any trouble lately, Caleb?" Elliot asked with sudden seriousness.

Caleb shook his head. "Not with poachers. We did run into some stillers though—back up in the swamps. It would have been right down your alley, Elliot. We chopped up that still like a regular vice squad. And I told them I have a friend in Texas who would just love to come over and kick their—er—" he cast Eve an apologetic look "—butts if I caught them making any more sour mash."

Elliot grimaced. "A lot of good that would do. Some more will eventually come along and do the same thing."

Caleb darted him a disgusted look. "Yeah, Elliot," he drawled. "That's about the way it works. That's why you and I wear badges so we can do something about it."

"That's why you wear a badge, Caleb," Elliot pointed out. "Mine is in there in a drawer, and it's beginning to like it in there. It never gets hit, kicked, threatened or shot at. It never gets accused or cussed at, or spit on. It doesn't have to prove itself to anyone. Yeah, it's beginning to like it more and more each day."

Caleb snorted and tugged his hat down onto his forehead. "Sounds pretty damn boring to me," he told Elliot, then threw Eve another sheepish smile. "Sorry, Miss Eve, Elliot always brings out my bad language."

Eve noticed Elliot's eyes narrow on the game

ranger. "I believe, Caleb," he said slowly, "you'd better answer your radio. Someone over in Sabine parish is wanting you."

Caleb Jones must have realized he couldn't push things any further with Elliot than he already had. Eve wondered if the man knew what had happened to Elliot back in Fort Worth. She had a suspicion that he did. In fact, if she were a betting person, she'd say Caleb was one of the very few people Elliot was close to.

"You're probably right," he said, sauntering toward his truck. "It's amazing what a popular guy I am around here." He turned and saluted Eve with a forefinger at the brim of his Stetson. "Pleasure meeting you, Miss Eve. And why don't you make Elliot see he needs to pin that badge back on. He's getting damn soft back here in these woods."

Eve merely smiled as Caleb went out the gate and hopped into his pickup. After he'd turned around and taken off down the road in a cloud of dust, Elliot cussed softly under his breath.

"He irritates the hell out of me."

Eve's smile deepened. "You like him, Elliot. I'd even go so far as to say he's been your best friend for years."

"Hmm," Elliot grunted. "Caleb's been Lord over there in Louisiana so long, the authority's gone to his head."

Eve leaned back on her palms and laughed softly. "You should have told him that," she dared him.

The frown disappeared from Elliot's face. He looked at Eve and smiled faintly. "No, I shouldn't have—not seriously, that is. Caleb is one man I don't like to tangle with. When we were growing up, we fought like cats and dogs, and neither one of us was ever sure about beating the other. I'm too old to see which one of us could whip the other now."

Eve leaned over and scratched Rebel between the ears. The dog whined with pleasure, and Eve said thoughtfully, "He wants you to go back to being a cop."

Elliot snorted. "That's all I've heard out of him since I came back. Caleb lives in a different world. He thinks because he likes what he does, I should like what I do."

"Did you both go into law enforcement at the same time?" she asked curiously.

Elliot nodded, and a wistful look suddenly crossed his face. "Yes, we did." Abruptly he stood and reached down for her hand.

Eve took it and allowed him to pull her to her feet. She knew he wanted to change the subject. Eve could understand that up to a point, but she was beginning to wonder if he planned on always keeping that part of his life away from her.

"Are you ready for a swim?"

She nodded, and he smiled and leaned down and kissed her lips. Her sigh of pleasure caressed his face as he pulled back and looked at her.

"Let me go get my things from the truck," she told him.

Elliot waited for her to change, and while she did, Eve realized it had been a while since she'd taken time off to swim. Sometimes she and her friend Julie, from Zwolle, would go together. But that had been ages ago.

Eve's tank suit was pink and black, and she covered it with a pink oversized T-shirt. When she came out of the bathroom, Elliot whistled at the sight of her legs. Yet Eve hardly noticed the appreciation on his face. She was too busy looking back at him standing there in nothing but a pair of faded cutoffs.

He had heavily muscled legs, tanned and covered

with fine black hair. They were a royal finish to the rest of his body, and she wondered if she could possibly look as good to him as he did to her.

Swallowing, she smiled and met his eyes. "I'm as white as the inside of a cream can, so don't look at me too closely," she warned.

Chuckling, he curled his arm around her waist and led her out of the house. "I love cream, Eve. It's smooth and rich and very good."

The sun was peeping back and forth between the clouds as they walked over the trail that led down to the pond. Rebel trotted in front of them, sniffing the way.

Just as they topped the rise of the pond bank, Eve ran eagerly ahead of him and out onto the dock. Quickly shedding her top, she flashed Elliot an impish grin, then jumped over the edge.

She came up spluttering and wiping hair out of her eyes. Elliot sat on the edge of the dock, watching her with an indulgent smile.

"I take it you like the water?" he asked.

His legs dangled over the edge of the dock. Eve closed her hands around his ankles and pulled herself closer to him so that each muscled calf was on either side of her face.

"I love the water. Don't you remember, I'd been out on the water when you met me?"

Did she imagine he could ever forget that night? He'd never been so entranced by any woman as he had been by her that night. Even now the simple touch of her fingers on his legs was a sweet distraction.

"Yes, I do remember, Eve," he said huskily, then added, "You could have been killed in the fog."

She pulled a face at him. "You and Rebel saved me."

His eyes traveled over her slim arms and softly rounded breasts. "Does that mean you belong to me now?"

"I'd like to think so," she said gently, then, with a low laugh, she tugged hard on his legs.

The unexpected movement caught him off guard, and he tumbled forward, knocking Eve beneath the water with his falling weight.

They came up at the same time, Eve laughing and Elliot coughing.

"Oh, Elliot, you had the funniest look of panic on your face," she said, unable to stem her laughter.

He swiped his black hair away from his face and lunged for Eve. "You really are a little imp, Eve Crawford. And I think you need to pay—"

"Elliot!" she squealed as his strong hands grabbed around her waist. "Don't dunk me! I can't stand it!"

His hazel eyes glittered over her wet face, then down to where her suit veed deeply between her breasts.

"Come here, honey," he said in a gently coaxing voice. "I won't dunk you, I promise."

Eve kept a wary eye on his face as she allowed him to pull her closer.

"You look like you would," she said with suspicion.

"Eve, darlin', I wouldn't do something you didn't like. Now come here," he drawled huskily. "I have another kind of payment in mind for you."

Grinning, she pushed into him and wound her arms around his neck. His wet mouth covered hers instantly, and Eve kissed him back with wanton hunger.

His hands splayed across her bottom and tugged her up against him. She lifted her feet and wound her legs around his, allowing him and the buoyancy of the water to keep her afloat.

"Mmm, that was some payment," Elliot murmured, his nose nuzzling her cheek. His hand slid upward and tightened around her waist.

"I'm glad you liked it, Mr. Elliot. Am I forgiven now?" she asked sweetly.

His forehead leaned into hers, and his mouth drew closer to brush soft, teasing kisses across her lips.

Eve moaned, her hands clinging to his shoulders as she waited eagerly for him to deepen the kiss. She was drunk from his touch, and barely registered when he began to lift her up and away from him.

Only when he pulled his mouth away from hers and flashed her a wicked grin did she realize what he was going to do, but by then it was too late.

"No, you're not forgiven," he growled with a laugh, then heaved her up and tossed her backwards.

Eve shrieked as she went under the water, but she surfaced laughing and splashing his face with water.

They played and swam for the next hour. Eve was a strong swimmer, but by the time they dragged themselves back up onto the dock she was exhausted.

Spreading a towel beneath the shade of a willow, she stretched out on it and waited for the heat to dry her.

Elliot toweled his thick hair, then sat down beside Eve. She looked at him with loving eyes. He reached over and slid his palm down the top of her thigh.

It touched and humbled him to know that she had not given herself to any man, but that she would gladly bestow him that honor.

She was pure and good, two things that had been lacking in his life for a long time, and it made Elliot realize how much he'd missed those qualities in the people who'd surrounded him.

His eyes locked with her gray ones. Slowly his hand slid upward and rested on her flat stomach.

"I love you, Eve," he said abruptly.

For long moments, Eve merely studied his face. Then tears formed in her eyes and spilled onto her cheeks.

"Oh, Elliot."

It was all she could say. Her throat was too thick with love and emotion to say more.

Elliot swallowed, wondering if his heart would burst with the love he felt for her. He reached up to touch her face, wondering why God thought him worthy of this woman.

"I guess you never expected to hear that from me," he whispered.

Eve's eyes held on to his. "I only hoped," she confessed.

His fingers reverently traced her cheekbone and outlined her lips.

"Before I met you I thought I was dead. I thought my life was over. You've given it all back to me, Eve."

She reached up and curled her hand around his forearm. "You're giving me too much credit, Elliot."

Slowly he lowered his head, slid his hands into her wet hair, and lifted her face up to his. "I'm giving you all the credit, Eve," he murmured before taking her mouth with his.

It was growing dusky, and oppressively still and humid by the time they returned to the house. The clouds had thickened, and in the far distance to the south and west, lightning streaked the darkening sky.

Elliot cooked a supper of warmed-up brown beans and corn bread for Eve. They ate it out on the screened-in back porch, where Elliot had set a little round table and added a candle in the middle. Eve insisted it was the best meal she'd ever eaten.

Earlier, she had changed into a pair of white shorts and a red blouse, and had plaited her wet hair into a French braid. She looked very fresh and young in the candlelight. Elliot couldn't take his eyes off her. He'd known beautiful women in the past, some perhaps with faces more perfect than Eve's. But none of them could equal her loveliness, he thought. She glowed from the inside, a glow that showed in her eyes, her smile and her laughter.

"Whatever made you think you wanted to be a lawyer, Eve?" he asked curiously.

She watched Elliot slather a hunk of corn bread with butter and grape jam, which he'd announced beforehand was going to be their dessert.

"It's something that's always interested me. From the time I was old enough to even partially understand the workings of the law, I've followed every trial that was ever in the paper, or on the TV news. I suppose the fact that my mother was killed added to my interest. Someone took her life and kept going. They were never caught, never made to pay for what they did to her. I've never been able to accept that."

Elliot felt every word she was saying because he'd seen tragedy from both sides. He knew the tearing emotions it produced.

"I can understand that. But if you're only doing it for revenge, then you'll never get anything out of it."

Eve shook her head as she broke a piece of corn bread down the middle. "I'm not doing it for revenge. All I want is justice—for both sides, guilty or innocent."

Elliot felt a spark kindle inside him at her words. She was echoing all the beliefs that he'd fought for in the past.

"That's good. As long as it works that way," he told her.

She spread some butter and jam on the corn bread, then took a bite and chewed it slowly. "Dedicated people can make it work. It's obvious that the stronger our legal system is, the stronger our cities and communities will be. I'd like to know that I'm contributing to that."

Elliot finished off his corn bread, then wiped his mouth on a napkin. "You do that just by paying taxes."

"That's not enough for me. And I'm almost certain it's not enough for you."

"Eve—" he began in frustration.

Not wanting to sound like she was nagging or harping, Eve rose quickly from her chair and started to the kitchen. "Do I get coffee?" she asked cheerfully.

"I'll make it," he said, tossing down his napkin and following her.

By the time the coffee had perked, a storm had started to brew. Elliot and Eve sat on a swing out on the back porch and watched the rain and lightning come closer and closer.

"Do you think it will create a tornado?" she asked him.

"No. But if it gets worse, we'll go down in the cellar."

"You have a cellar?"

"Behind the smokehouse," he told her. He watched Eve sip her coffee. "Why, are you frightened of storms?"

"Only when they get really bad," she admitted.

He put his arm around her and snuggled her closer to him. Eve rested her cheek against his white T-shirt.

"I wouldn't let anything happen to you, honey."

Smiling to herself, she said, "I know you wouldn't, Elliot. I feel very safe with you." Which was certainly true, she thought. She instinctively knew that Elliot was a protector, a man who'd never turn away from danger.

"Eve," he said suddenly, "I want to marry you."

Stunned, she lifted her head and looked at him. Finally she managed to speak.

"Just like that?"

He grinned at her amazed expression. "Just like that," he repeated. "Are you going to say yes?"

She could see that in spite of his outwardly light attitude, he was completely serious.

"Say yes? Elliot—I—I've been telling myself that you're not the kind of man who'd want to marry and—"

"I wasn't the kind of man who wanted to marry," he put in, "until I met you."

"Oh, Elliot," she breathed, not knowing what to think. She loved him so much, and she wanted nothing more than to marry him, to belong to him in every sense. But there were so many unsaid things between them. "You can't be sure about this."

His eyes held hers. "Does that mean you don't want to marry me?"

She shook her head and felt herself begin to tremble. "I would love to marry you—if—if—"

"If what?"

"What about my plans for law school?"

"If that's what you really want, I'll stand behind you on it. I don't want you to sacrifice your dreams for me. I just want you to share your life with me."

Happiness flooded through her. She'd never expected

him to react this way. It gave her hope that he was having second thoughts about his career.

"Oh, Elliot, you can't know how much that means to me."

One side of his mouth cocked upward, and he pulled her against him and kissed her with a sweetness that melted Eve's heart.

"You can't know how much you mean to me, Eve," he murmured against her cheek.

"Does this mean that you've had a change of heart? That you're ready to go back to Fort Worth and get on with your life?"

He lifted her slightly away from him and from the look on his face, Eve would have thought she'd just shot him.

"No," he said, and Eve caught the rueful note in his voice. It tore at her heart. "I decided last night after I took you home that I'm going to resign. I'm going to drive to Fort Worth next week and turn my badge and gun over to my captain and tell him my decision."

"Elliot, no!"

"What do you mean no? This doesn't have anything to do with our getting married."

Appalled by his words, she pulled away from him and got to her feet. Crossing the porch, she stood with her back to him. The storm had reached them. Eve watched the jagged streaks of lightning tear up the sky while thinking it couldn't begin to match the turmoil in her heart.

"I can't believe you really think that."

Rain began to fall, drumming loudly on the tin roof. She didn't hear Elliot when he walked up behind her.

"Eve," he said in a gentler tone, "my being a cop is

in the past. I want to put that behind me. I want to start fresh—with you."

Tears smarted the back of Eve's eyes as she turned to face him. "That would be fine if I thought your being a cop was over. But I—I don't think that's the case."

Groaning, he closed his eyes and speared one hand through the side of his dark hair.

"Why do you women always think you know what's better for a man than he does?" He opened his eyes to glare at her. "You don't know about my past, Eve. So how could you possibly know what's best for me?"

Her breast rose as she drew in a deep breath. "That's just it," she said with a shake of her head. "I don't know about your past. You're asking me to be your wife, but if you can't share yourself with me now, what kind of marriage would we have?"

His eyes grew stormy-green. He turned away from Eve and linked his hands in a helpless gesture at the back of his neck. "Eve," he said in a carefully controlled voice. "I'm not asking you to give me a past history of your life. I'm willing to take you as you are. Why do you ask more from me? You said you trusted me, believed in me. Obviously that wasn't true."

Thunder cracked and rumbled around the house. Eve had the urge to clap her hands over her ears, but she didn't quite know if it was to shut out the storm, or to shut out Elliot's accusations.

Swallowing, she stepped toward him. "I do believe in you, Elliot, with everything inside of me. I also know you better than you think, and I can see that whatever happened to you in the past is still controlling your future."

"I'm trying to get away from my past, Eve. Can't you see that? I've rehashed it over and over for months. I'll be damned if I have to keep rehashing it with you!"

Eve was suddenly shaking with anger. She loved him but he still wanted to shut her out. Somehow she had to make him see how she felt.

"Elliot, if you don't want to go back to the police force, then what are you going to do with your life?"

He shrugged. "I'll find something. I can drive a truck, or maybe get on at the sawmill over at Zwolle."

Eve hardly ever swore, but she did now. "And you think you'd be happy doing that?" she asked in angry amazement. "You'd be happy working your butt off for practically nothing—"

"Oh, so that's it," he growled. "You're not really worried about me—you're worried about the money and whether I could support you—"

That did it for Eve. With a cutting glare, she marched around him and started through the house.

"Where are you going?" Elliot demanded, quickly following behind her.

"I'm going home," she said, her voice daring him to try and stop her.

Elliot put a hand on her slender shoulder and spun her around to face him. "How do you propose to get there?"

"I'll drive your Jeep. You certainly don't need it, anyway. All you want to do is stay here in the woods and feel sorry for yourself!"

Elliot's eyes glittered dangerously. Eve knew she'd angered him, and probably hurt him even more. But she was beyond hand-holding with Elliot; she couldn't pretend with him.

"I don't know why I thought you were different from the rest," he bit out in a self-accusing voice.

Eve shrugged away from his grasp. "Because I *am* different," she tossed back at him, her chin thrust out, her eyes blazing. "I'm different because I love you."

Her words were enough to wash the anger from his face. Even so, there was still anguish in his eyes as he reached for her again.

Eve allowed him to pull her against him, and she had to fight not to cry as she pressed her cheek against his chest.

"Eve, I can't believe we're fighting because I asked you to marry me," he said after a few moments.

Eve closed her eyes and listened to his heartbeat. "Elliot, I just can't let you throw away your career. All that training—the work and dedication you've put into it the past ten years is not something you just toss out the window like a piece of wadded paper."

His fingers were in her hair, sliding from the crown to the waves lying against her shoulders. "I'm trying to tell you that I *want* to toss it out."

Eve shook her head back and forth against his chest. "I don't believe you. I saw the look on your face when Caleb was talking about those moonshiners."

"Oh, hell, what do a few penny-ante moonshiners have to do with anything!" he retorted.

"Because they're lawbreakers," she reasoned. "And it's in you to go after lawbreakers, just like it's in Rebel to go after a coon in the woods."

Elliot closed his eyes and swallowed at the emotion welling up in his throat. Why was she doing this? Why was she forcing him to look at things that he'd fought so hard to forget?

"Eve, if you only knew what I'd been through you'd—"

Her head tilted up to look at his face. "All you have to do is tell me, Elliot," she invited. "Maybe if I knew I would change my mind. Maybe I would say chuck it all and stay here in east Texas."

His hazel eyes studied her face while he imagined how it would be to pour it all out to her. It would be like ridding himself of handcuffs. The relief would be great. But not if it caused him to lose Eve. That was a cost he couldn't pay. He'd rather remain shackled than not have Eve in his life.

"Eve, darlin', can't you understand that it's ugly?"

"I can deal with that, Elliot. I'm stronger than you think."

That was exactly what Elliot knew. She was a strong-minded woman. She might just decide she didn't want to get tied up with someone like him.

"I—I'm just not ready to lay all that open, Eve."

Her gray eyes were sad as she slowly shook her head. "Then I don't think you're ready to marry me, Elliot."

He wanted to argue, but he knew from the expression in her eyes that they would only go around in circles.

Instead, he got the keys to the Jeep and drove her home. When she leaned over and kissed him good-night, he held her tightly.

"I love you, Eve. You do believe that, don't you?"

She looked into his eyes and trailed her fingers across his cheek. "Yes, I believe you love me," she told him.

"But you won't marry me?"

Her heart ached with regret. "Not now. Not like this."

She slipped out of his arms and climbed from the Jeep. "Good night, Elliot."

As Eve walked toward the house, tears burned her eyes and cheeks. Yet she didn't look back. She couldn't trust herself to.

Chapter Eight

Several hours later, Eve pushed back the twisted sheet and swung her legs over the side of the bed.

She was as wide-awake now as she was when she'd first gone to bed. Thoughts of Elliot zoomed through her head like a roller coaster out of control.

Everything was happening so fast. Eve thought love was something that would come gradually— falling in love with Elliot had proved how wrong that idea had been.

Thrusting back her tousled hair, she rose to her feet, then pulled on a thin robe. Fast or slow, she thought, it had happened, and now he said he wanted to marry her. What was she going to do?

Groaning with frustration, Eve left her bedroom and groped her way through the darkness to the kitchen. Once there, she poured herself a glass of orange juice.

Eve stood at the kitchen sink sipping slowly and looking out the window. The rain was still falling, but not as heavily as it had been when Elliot had brought her home.

She wondered if he'd made it home safely, and whether he was still awake. Was he walking through the rooms of that old house, still angry with her and telling himself she wasn't worth the frustration?

Tears stung Eve's eyes. She closed them and rubbed her fingers across the burning lids. *Oh, Elliot, I love you so,* she thought desperately. *I don't want to hurt you, I just want you to be happy. Happy with yourself and happy with me.*

Across the lake, Elliot drove eastward into Louisiana. Rain pelted the windshield, forcing him to keep the wipers on high speed.

He'd started home after he'd left Eve's house, but after a couple of miles he had turned around and headed across Pendleton bridge and into Louisiana.

Emotions burned inside him like a strong drink of whiskey, and Elliot knew it would be impossible to sleep.

Almost an hour and a half later, Elliot turned off the main highway and drove down a short lane canopied with tall pines and huge magnolia trees.

The house was dark, but Elliot knew Caleb was there. His truck was parked out front.

He climbed the two rock steps, walked across the planked porch, then banged loudly on the screen door.

When Caleb failed to answer, Elliot tried the door. To his disgust, he found both of them unlocked.

As he entered the house, Elliot thought it would serve his friend right to scare the hell out of him. But

Elliot knew Caleb would have his gun near, and he wasn't too fond of the idea of getting shot. Once was enough.

"Caleb, get up."

Elliot stood at the bedroom door and watched Caleb stir beneath the white sheet.

"Elliot," he growled sleepily, quickly rising to a sitting position. "What the hell are you doing?"

"Get up. Let's go drink a beer."

Caleb reached over and switched on a bedside lamp. "Are you crazy? It's after midnight and it's pouring rain."

"So? You've had enough beauty sleep. And I want a beer."

Caleb threw back the sheet and reached for his jeans lying in a heap on the floor. "And I suppose it would make too much sense to drink one at home."

"I'm not in a sensible mood tonight," Elliot said sourly.

Caleb looked at his friend. Now that the fog of sleep had cleared from his eyes, he could see that Elliot was troubled. Quickly he shrugged into a shirt and jerked on his boots.

"Lead the way, old buddy," Caleb said, slapping Elliot on the shoulder.

Elliot drove them to Natchitoches, to a little bar on a quiet side street.

Once they were inside and the bartender had set two mugs of draft beer in front of them, Caleb said, "Okay, Elliot, you've been quiet long enough. What happened? You heard from your captain or something?"

Elliot's lips twisted ruefully as he reached for his beer. "Or something," he muttered. "I asked Eve to marry me."

Caleb stared at Elliot. "Marry you?" he repeated in a stunned voice. "I never thought I'd hear you even breathe the word."

Elliot tried to laugh, but it came out more like a bitter snort. "Well, you have now. Not that it's done any good. She turned me down. Isn't that a hell of a note? Before, there wasn't a woman alive who could have hog-tied me and dragged me to the altar. And now—"

He shook his head, leaving the sentence dangling with uncertainty.

"Well," Caleb said carefully, "she must have given you a reason. From what I saw today, she was looking at you like there wasn't another man on earth."

Elliot swallowed more of the beer before he said grimly, "She gave me a reason all right. It's because of Fort Worth. That mess is following me—"

"You told her about it?"

"No. Yes. I mean—I told her there'd been trouble and I'd taken a leave of absence. But that's all."

"Well, hell, Elliot."

Elliot glared at Caleb. "'Well, hell, Elliot,' what? What does that mean?"

"It means, man, that you should have told her. You can't expect to marry her and keep something like that from her—"

"I don't want her to know," Elliot burst out in a low growl. "I want her to respect me. I want her to be proud of me. You think she will be once I drop all that garbage on her?"

Caleb shook his head, smiling faintly. "You do have it bad, don't you?"

"Caleb," Elliot warned, "I'm not in any mood for your bull—"

"All right. All right," Caleb soothed, holding up his palm.

Elliot let out a pent-up breath, then stared down at the sudsy foam on his beer. After a moment, he said in a dismal voice, "I'm afraid I'm going to lose her."

"Why?"

"She thinks I should go back to Fort Worth. She has this crazy idea in her head that I still want to be a cop. Hell, she doesn't know anything about it! How could she know what I want or need?"

Caleb shook his head. "All women are that way. They always think they know what's best for us men. That's funny, you know, because I don't think us men ever know about women."

"Amen," Elliot muttered.

"So. What are you going to do?"

"I don't know. I've never been so mixed up in my life."

"Well, I know one thing. She has the prettiest gray eyes I've ever seen. But then, eyes aren't everything," Caleb said thoughtfully. "'Course, she has nice hair, too. Dark, long and soft. But then, you can find a dark-haired woman on every corner."

He reached over and gave Elliot an encouraging slap on the back. "I wouldn't worry about it, buddy. You'll find another one."

Elliot didn't want another one. He never would. "Not like Eve," he said.

"Sounds to me like you wouldn't want to find one like her anyway. She's bossy and demanding. Wanting you to tell her all about yourself like that, wanting you to be a cop when you could probably make her a fine living hauling pulpwood for old man Simms. She's really got some nerve, Elliot. Why, I bet Simms would pay you at least thirty dollars a day. A woman couldn't ask for more than that. Who does she think she is, wanting you to go back to being a lieutenant? Doesn't she know you might get shot at?"

"You've been shot at," Elliot retorted, deliberately ignoring the rest of Caleb's condescending speech.

Caleb grinned broadly. "Yeah. But I like it. It gets the old blood pumping."

"You think I'm afraid of being shot at?"

"No," Caleb said, with sudden seriousness. "I think you're more afraid of losing the woman you love."

"Then what do you propose I do?" Elliot asked tersely.

Caleb shrugged, a helpless expression on his face. "You're asking me? I've never been in love."

Elliot frowned at him. "You've really been a big help, Caleb. I drive seventy miles over here to see you, and you make me feel just as bad as I did when I started."

After a few moments of silence, Caleb slapped his palm loudly down on the polished bar, making the sleepy guy at the end nearly fall off his seat.

"I've got it, Elliot! You're just going to have to go to Eve and tell her the whole story. After she hears it, she'll see that she's just asking too much of you to go on being a cop. She'll say she's sorry she ever mentioned it in the first place. You can get married and all's well that ends well. You might as well go tomorrow and see Old Man Simms about the pulpwood job—"

Elliot jabbed a finger in Caleb's face. "Shut up about Old Man Simms and the pulpwood—"

"I was just trying to help, Elliot," Caleb said innocently, but had to turn his head to keep Elliot from seeing the smug smile on his face.

"You're trying to be a pain in the rear as usual," Elliot barked. "And you're doing a heck of a job at it."

Caleb laughed. "Drink up, Lieutenant. It's almost breakfast time. And I just hate warm beer for breakfast."

Early the next morning, Eve was at the motel going through paperwork when a car sounded outside.

She reached over and pushed up the slatted blind covering the window to see Elliot's Jeep. Her heart began to thud as she watched him climb down from the wheel.

He headed toward the restaurant, and Eve hurried to the door to call to him.

"I'm over here, Elliot."

Elliot turned instantly at the sound of Eve's voice. She was standing in the doorway dressed in a pair of blue jeans and bright red blouse. It was amazing how beautiful she looked to him.

As he walked across the lawn toward Eve, she noticed he was wearing the same jeans and T-shirt he had on the previous night. His face was unshaven and shadowed with prickly black stubble. His eyes were bleary and red, as if he hadn't been asleep at all.

"You're out early," she commented once he reached the door.

"I spent the night over at Caleb's, and he had to go out early," he explained.

"Oh. I see." Eve had thought maybe he'd been awake all night worrying about their differences. Maybe he hadn't been as hurt over her turning down his proposal as she'd first believed.

He entered the office, and Eve shut the door behind him. Walking back to her desk, she sat down on the corner and lifted her face to him.

"I was just doing some paperwork. Would you like a cup of coffee?"

He shook his head. "I wanted to see if you could get away for the day."

"For the day?" she repeated blankly.

He looked at her and felt his insides crumble. "Yes. I'm ready to talk, Eve. Really talk. If you're ready to listen."

Elliot's husky words pulled at her heart. She hadn't expected him to make such an offer. Not after last night.

Closing the distance between them, Eve reached for his hand. Squeezing it, she said, "Just let me call over to the kitchen to let Marcia know I'll be out."

Once they were outside and settled in the Jeep, Elliot asked, "Where would you like to go?"

Eve looked at him. "It doesn't matter. Anywhere you like."

Elliot started the motor and drove back out to the main highway. There he headed south across Patroon bridge. When they reached a crossroads, he turned toward Louisiana.

Eve sat quietly in her seat, taking in the muddy lake water as the Jeep sped across the three-mile Pendleton bridge that connected Texas and Louisiana. The rotted tree trunks dotting the water were stark and lonely-looking. Eve thought they matched the feeling in her heart.

It was still cloudy from the night's rain. The air was heavy and hot, and water lay in puddles on the red ground and the uneven spots in the highway.

About a quarter of a mile after they entered Louisiana, Elliot turned on the directional signal and headed down a small blacktopped road that led to Merritt Mountain Park.

The road wound through the dense woods for two or

three miles, and they traveled it in silence. They met no cars along the way, and when Elliot parked near the Tom Sawyer Boat Chapel, the place seemed silent and empty.

This had always been one of Eve's favorite spots. The boat was a replica of a three-deck steamboat and was used for nondenominational church services and other group activities. Huge cypress and hardwood trees draped with Spanish moss shaded its deck. Eve couldn't summon up much enjoyment at seeing the unique structure today.

"Let's walk over to the church," Elliot suggested once he'd parked the Jeep and shut off the motor.

Eve nodded and joined him on the other side of the vehicle. They walked slowly, and along the way Eve tried to listen to the bird chatter and the faint breeze in the treetops instead of the nervous beat of her heart.

But it was impossible for her to remain calm and unaffected. She somehow knew that whatever Elliot was about to tell her would make a difference in their lives. She just didn't know if it would be for better or worse.

The paddleboat possessed three decks. The main deck was built of glass walls and filled with seats, but since it was a hot morning Eve and Elliot chose to remain outside and lean against the rail instead of going inside.

For long moments they stood close together, Eve not wanting to question him, and Elliot not knowing where to start.

Finally he said, "I guess I've gone about this all wrong," he finally said. "I guess I should have told you about myself right from the start."

Eve smiled faintly as her eyes lovingly touched his face, the hawkish nose, the scar on his lip, the deep green color of his eyes. "You didn't much like me at first. I irritated you and made you want a cigarette."

Elliot smiled halfheartedly. "I thought you were beautiful."

He said it with such sweet conviction that Eve blushed and looked down at her hands.

She remembered how kind he'd been that night and how badly she'd wanted him to make love to her. That hadn't changed. She wanted to live with him, marry him, love him for the rest of her life.

When she looked back up at him, everything she was feeling was in her eyes. "I don't want to pry things from you, Elliot. If you're not ready to tell me—"

He touched her lips with his fingertips. "Don't stop me, Eve. Because if you do, I may not have the courage to go on."

It was impossible for Eve to imagine Elliot without courage. She knew he had probably faced danger many times since he'd lived the life of a cop. But she supposed there was at least one time in every man's life when he felt battered down by something.

She merely nodded with understanding. Elliot drew in a breath, pushed his palms down the thighs of his jeans, then propped his elbows on the railing

"There'd been a series of cattle thefts," he started. "On several ranches just outside the city. It wasn't just penny-ante business, a cow here or a bull there. It was major thefts. Tractor-trailer rigs filled and hauled away in the night."

"You're talking about lots of money," Eve replied.

"An enormous amount," he agreed. "And this went on for several months. The investigating officers that were on the case didn't seem to be getting anywhere.

The ranchers were screaming bloody murder for something to be done. The chief was coming down hard on my captain to get results. I usually worked inner city, and at the time I was working on an illegal firearm case. But he pulled me off it and told me he wanted me to go undercover on the rustling problem."

"And what did you say?" Eve asked

"I told him that concrete and back alleys was more my style than pastures and country roads."

"He made you do it anyway," Eve guessed.

"Right. I didn't have any choice in the matter," Elliot told her.

"Is that the way you usually worked? Undercover, I mean."

Elliot shook his head. "Only if a case cropped up that we couldn't make any headway with. I usually only worked as a plainclothes investigator. But this time the captain thought we needed more to crack this particular case."

Eve studied him earnestly. "Well, did you crack it?"

A bitter sneer marred his face. "In the end—no. Not completely."

He turned to face her, and Eve's heart lurched at the torment she saw in his eyes.

"I was suspended from the force and put under a grand jury investigation."

His words were like heavy stones dropping in a pool of water. Eve stared at him while the aftershock washed over her.

"You? Elliot! I can't believe that!"

He thrust his fingers through his hair, raking it restlessly back from his forehead. "Neither could I, Eve. At least not while it was happening."

Eve didn't know what to say. She had expected to hear him say that his partner had been killed, or someone he'd once respected had gone against the law. She'd never expected something like this.

"But surely—I can't understand, Elliot. I know you— I know you couldn't have done anything wrong. Why—"

"It's a long story," he interrupted.

Her expression was gentle as she looked at him. "We have all day, Elliot. And I'd really like to listen."

Elliot had grown so used to people looking at him with accusation and suspicion that Eve's complete faith amazed him.

"If I went into detail it would take all day. To make a long story short, I had to work for a month before I got even a small breakthrough. But then things gradually began to piece together. I discovered that the thefts had been carried out by a well-organized bunch, the leader of which lived somewhere near Brownsville. The cattle were stolen, then hauled across the border into New Mexico and sold to different feedlots."

Eve's brows drew thoughtfully together. "But surely they could be identified as stolen. What about brands and—"

"Some ranchers don't brand now, and many use only earmarks. It saves lots of time and work."

"But these cattle," Eve went on, "their sale had to be consigned by some ranch or someone—"

Elliot admired her intelligent observation. "They were," he said. "By a fictitious ranch. One of the men would pick up the check from the feedlot and deposit it in a bank in Dallas under the same fictitious name. The leader would then collect it and split the profit."

"Sounds like they had plenty of nerve. You would

think they would rather have taken the cattle to Mexico, where the sale would have been harder to trace," Eve mused aloud.

Elliot frowned and shook his head. "You're right about one thing, Eve. These guys had lots of nerve. And in the end, I discovered why. Two officers were involved. They were paving them an easy access road to the cattle and anything else they needed."

"Oh, Elliot, no!" Eve gasped.

His mouth tightened. "I'd gotten in so deep that the thieves had accepted me into their own little circle. I posed as a truck driver, and they hired me to drive the stolen cattle. The night a big job was supposed to be pulled, I had an uneasy feeling that something wasn't right. They wanted me to handle the money this time. But as the time grew closer, I told myself not to get spooked, they trusted me. And if I hung on just a little longer, I could get enough on them to put the whole damn bunch away, even the ringleader."

"I suppose all this took a long time," Eve mused aloud.

"Too long," Elliot said with a sigh. "I was tired of the whole thing. I just wanted to get it over with. I hadn't been home to sleep in my own bed for over eight weeks. I couldn't go near the department, my friends, or anything connected to my normal life. I was living out that one case, and I wanted to put an end to it. So I turned a deaf ear to my uneasiness."

"Something or someone tipped them off to who you really were," Eve guessed.

Elliot looked away from her and stared out at the moss-draped woods. "It was me, inadvertently. I contacted a sergeant in vice, whom I thought could be trusted. He assured me that he'd contact our captain and that officers would be there for a raid when the theft took place."

Eve found she was practically holding her breath, waiting for his next words.

"Were they?" she asked

"When we picked up the cattle, no one was there. I knew something was wrong, but there was nothing for me to do but carry them on to the feedlot. I had the money in my pocket and had just crossed back into Texas when the law stopped us at a weigh station. The two guys with me pulled out guns and started shooting. Things got messy and chaotic then. In the end I was wounded in the leg."

Eve's face blanched white. "What about the other two men with you?"

His mouth thinned to a grim line. "Somehow they conveniently got away. And I was left holding the check and looking as guilty as hell. But that's not all. While I was in the hospital recuperating from the gunshot, I was told I'd been put under investigation. The police had discovered a large amount of cash in my house, along with several cattle sales receipts."

There was a fierce look of outrage on Eve's face. "They set you up, for God's sake!"

He shrugged. "The grand jury came to that same conclusion after its investigation. In the end they cleared me of any wrongdoing. But the damage had already been done. By that time most of my friends believed I was guilty and turned their backs on me."

"What about your captain?" she asked.

Elliot rubbed his face with both hands and let out a

deep sigh. Eve knew it must have cost him terribly to tell her all this.

"He wouldn't accept my badge and gun when I tried to resign. I'd worked under him for six years. He regarded me as a good officer and a friend. If it wasn't for him I would have chucked it all when I left Fort Worth."

Eve could now see why Elliot had such a bitter attitude toward the law. But she didn't understand why he was still letting the whole thing dictate his life.

Elliot looked at her. Was she seeing him in a different way now? Would she be like the rest and say he'd been a cop on the take?

"You should be thankful for him," Eve said.

"Why do you say that?"

"Because you would have regretted it if you'd impulsively resigned."

Elliot shifted around so that he was facing her straight on. "Eve, are you saying—you mean all that I've told you hasn't made you see anything differently?"

Frowning, Eve shook back the hair that had fallen in her face. "Of course it has, Elliot. I see lots of things now that I couldn't before. I see that before all this happened, you were happy being a cop. But now you're letting this incident mar everything."

"Hell, Eve," he muttered. "I wouldn't be much of a man if it hadn't marred me."

"That's true," Eve agreed. "But now it's time to get on with things."

"Meaning what?" he asked wearily.

She reached over and took hold of both is hands. "Elliot, you were a good, dedicated policeman. That same dedicated man is still there inside you, even if he is cloaked with bitterness. The way I see it, you have to go back to Fort Worth."

His hazel eyes glittered over her face. "Oh yeah?" he asked in a tone so dry it crackled. "You think I like being kicked?"

Eve's lip tightened to a thin, angry line. "If I've gotten things straight with this story, there're two men still on the force that shouldn't be there, right?"

"You mean Yates and Delvecchio? As far as I know they are. I knew they were guilty, but I had no way of proving it. All the evidence I had against them was circumstantial."

Eve's eyes widened. "The bullet in your leg. Didn't ballistics check it out?"

Elliot's face hardened like setting concrete. "It was from Yates's .38."

Eve gasped softly. "Well then, isn't that proof enough?"

Elliot snorted. "He had a feasible reason for shooting. I was in a gang of thieves. I merely got caught in the crossfire."

"Elliot! That's—you have to go back. Can't you see?"

His eyes were virtually blazing back at Eve. "Go back? Back to what?" he wanted to know.

She shook her head at him, amazed that he didn't see it as she did. "Don't you care that there're two men still on the force acting like honest lawmen, when actually they're not?"

He gripped her hands. "I was an honest lawman acting like I wasn't. But I was hauled out and roasted on a turning spit. Every part of my life was put on display as if I were the common criminal. If that's the way the department wants to work things, then fine.

They can stick with their rules and regulations. They can keep Yates and Delvecchio, they deserve them!"

"Elliot, you don't mean that," Eve argued. "I know that what they did to you was an injustice. But I know there's more to you than just slinking back here to east Texas and cowering down like a whipped hound."

"Who said anything about cowering?" he demanded hotly. "I'm not cowering—I'm quitting."

Eve pulled her hands away from his and walked to the end of the deck. She was so angry that tears burned her eyes and she was forced to grit her teeth to keep from screaming. She was angry at what they'd done to Elliot and to what it was now doing to them. Yet she was even angrier because he wasn't willing to fight back.

"If that's what you want then you're not the man I first thought you were," she said over her shoulder, keeping her back to him.

She heard him curse softly under his breath, then cross the space between them. When his hand touched her shoulder, she lifted her face to him.

There was a daring jut to her chin that made Elliot want to shake her. She was the most strong-minded, opinionated woman he'd ever run into. But damn, he loved her!

"I'm not the man you first knew," he tried to reason. "I'm different because of you, Eve. I've fallen in love with you. I want to make my life with you."

Eve's features softened at his words. Groaning, she turned and slid her palms up his chest as her eyes locked with his.

"I'm glad, so glad that you love me, Elliot," she whispered fervently. "But I want that love to last."

"It will last," he insisted, his voice gruff with emotion.

Eve shook her head. "Being away from the force has made a void in your life, Elliot, and I'm afraid you're using me to fill that void."

"I'm not using you," he ground out. "I'm loving you."

"Yes! For now, maybe. But how long will it last, Elliot? You have to have more in your life than just me."

"I'll have some kind of job," he told her.

"But will you be happy with it? Will you be proud and happy with yourself and what you're doing?" She shook her head and turned away from him. Tears spilled onto her cheeks, and she desperately wiped at them.

Moments passed and Elliot didn't say anything. Eve continued in a tearful voice, "You can't expect to be happy with someone if you're not that way with yourself—inside, where it really counts. And that's what I want for us, Elliot," she whispered hoarsely.

His hands curved warm and strong over the back of her shoulders. "You're asking a hell of a lot from me, Eve."

She sniffed and focused her bleary eyes on the woods just beyond them. "If you were a lesser man, I wouldn't ask anything of you. But you're not a lesser man, Elliot. You're tough and courageous. You have honor and integrity. And one of these days those things are going to rear up and demand that you go back to Fort Worth and stand your ground."

Elliot felt part of him respond hungrily to her words. She painted him as a strong man, the man he'd always strived to be. But then another hurt, belligerent side asked himself why he should have to prove himself to anyone.

"I guess you're saying you won't marry me," he said in frustration.

A sob caught in her throat, and Eve did her best to swallow it down.

"I guess that's what I'm saying," she echoed in a small, sad voice.

For a moment Elliot closed his eyes and struggled to keep from twisting her around and taking her in his arms.

"I told you once, Eve, that doing something just for revenge never works. If I went back to Fort Worth just to get Yates and Delvecchio, what would that prove?"

She turned and faced him once again. Surprise was on her face. "Elliot, that's not what I want—I figure sooner or later, with or without your help, those two men will get their due. I want you to go back for yourself. Not for revenge, not to prove yourself to anyone. I want you to go back for you. Because being a policeman is what you are, and nothing or no one should take that away from you."

Elliot groaned and stepped away from her. "I could be happy here, Eve. We could be happy if you'd just give us the chance."

"I wish I could believe that."

"You're a damn stubborn woman, Eve," he said suddenly.

She was stubborn! Eve had never seen such an obstinate man before!

Stepping around him, she hurried off the boat and toward the Jeep.

Elliot stalked after her. She was climbing into the Jeep when he caught up with her. "You know, Eve, in my business we call what you're doing to me blackmail."

Eve gasped angrily as he climbed into the Jeep and shut the door with enough muscle to make the whole vehicle shiver.

"You're not in the business anymore, remember?" she flung the reminder at him, unable to stem the resurgent anger inside her.

"Damn right, woman," he countered. "And I don't intend to be."

Eve jerked her head away from him and stared unseeingly out the open window. "And I don't intend to be your wife!"

Elliot started the Jeep and rammed the gear shift down in reverse. "I've been alone before, I'll survive," he bit out.

"Oh, yes, you'll survive," she snapped tearfully. "You've proved you're a survivor. You're just not a fighter."

He wheeled the Jeep around and shot up the road with a force that snapped Eve's head back.

"You want a fighter, huh? Then go get one out of the prize ring!"

Eve was suddenly weary of the whole thing. "Take me home, Elliot. Just take me home."

The remainder of the drive back to Pine Ridge was made in taut silence. Eve passed the time staring out the window, her heart aching, wondering how love could produce such anger.

When Elliot stopped the Jeep in front of the bungalow, Eve looked over at his stern profile.

"When will I see you again?" she asked.

His head turned, and Eve's eyes collided with his. The look in them was unyielding, and Eve felt her heart sink to an even lower depth.

"I think it would be pointless to see each other any more. Eve," he said. "I can't be what you want me to be."

Eve felt a rush of tears form behind her eyelids. She

reached for the door latch and quickly released it. After she'd climbed down to the ground, she looked back at him.

"No, you've got it wrong, Elliot. You can't be what you really want to be."

His mouth tightened as his eyes bored into hers. For a moment she thought he was going to say more.

When he didn't, Eve turned away from him and started toward the house. Elliot shoved the Jeep into forward gear and stepped on the gas.

Gravel and dust billowed in the wake of the Jeep, shrouding it from view. Yet that hardly mattered. Even if she'd wanted, Eve couldn't have watched Elliot leave. Her eyes were too blurred with hot, helpless tears.

Chapter Nine

A week later Eve sat on one of the boat docks, staring pensively out at the star-strung sky and the calm, shimmering lake.

The misery in her heart was reflected in her gray eyes. She missed Elliot terribly, and not even the beauty of the night could ease the ache inside her.

She hadn't seen him since their argument, and now that a week had passed, Eve was certain it was over between them. Or at least it was over for Elliot. It would never be over for her.

He'd said there would be no point in trying to continue their relationship. Every time she thought of his words, she felt her heart rip just a little bit more. Elliot was out of her life. All she could see in front of her now was a bleak emptiness.

Voices sounded behind her. She turned her head to

see her father waving to a couple who'd just moored their boat several stalls down from where Eve was sitting.

The couple had obviously had a good day fishing. Burl stopped to look over their catch. When the two finally went on their way, he continued on toward his daughter.

"What are you doing down here, girl? Aren't you going to have some of Marcia's barbecue?"

Eve shook her head. "I'm not hungry."

The big man squatted down on his haunches next to Eve. "You haven't been hungry all week," he said, concern on his face. "You're getting so skinny a puff of wind is going to come along and blow you away."

One side of Eve's mouth lifted a fraction. "I'm always skinny," she reasoned.

Burl sighed, took the cap off his head and slapped it softly against his palm. "You're still moping over Elliot, aren't you?"

Eve's face grew even more dismal as she nodded her head. "I can't help it, Daddy," she said in a strained voice. "I keep telling myself to forget him, but it just doesn't work." She looked over at her father. "I guess you were right. Elliot wound up hurting me after all."

Eve had told her father what had happened between Elliot and her. She'd explained the problems Elliot had been through in Fort Worth and how scarred the bitter experience had left him. Burl had listened quietly and sympathetically, yet he had not commented about Eve's view of the situation. Now she wondered what he was thinking.

"That was a father talking. I thought he might want to live with a woman, but not marry her. I was wrong about him. Obviously he cares a great deal for you. He did ask you to marry him," Burl gently reminded his daughter.

Eve's eyes burned with unshed tears. She looked down at her lap where her fingers were locked helplessly together. "Yes, and I turned him down."

Burl continued to study Eve's downcast face. "Are you regretting that?"

Eve groaned softly. She was so confused and hurting she didn't know what to do or where to turn for an answer. "I'm regretting losing Elliot, no matter how it happened. I love him. I wanted to marry him, live my life with him."

Burl was silent for a moment, then he said, "But you wanted to do it on your terms, Eve. Men get sort of edgy when you start trying to back them into a corner. We don't take kindly to it."

Eve's head jerked back up and shot her father a glaring look. "I wasn't trying to back Elliot into a corner! And I didn't want everything on my terms!" she argued. "I believe with all my heart that Elliot still wants to be a policeman. If I thought he'd be happy living here hauling logs or growing cotton, I'd say fine. But I just don't think that's the case. And marriage is too big a step to gamble with."

"Maybe a gamble would be worth it. As it is, you're losing out anyway."

"You think I should back down, don't you?" she asked with faint surprise. "You think I should let Elliot decide on his own, don't you?"

Burl snorted with annoyance. "The way I see it, you've approached this whole situation like a bull with horns. Did you ever stop to think that Elliot feels pressured? He's been through a hell of a lot. Now you've given him an ultimatum—go back to the force, or I won't marry you."

Is that what she'd done? Is that how Elliot had taken the things she'd said to him? Eve felt sick inside.

"Daddy," she whispered miserably. "I didn't give him an ultimatum. I just said I couldn't marry him like this—with his life still hanging in shreds since he left Fort Worth. I only wanted him to go back and face things once again, to make sure about what he really wanted out of his life. I was willing to wait until he decided one way or the other."

Burl stood and looked down at Eve. "Maybe you should go tell him that again, Eve. All men have their pride, honey. And I imagine Elliot's took a lot of battering when he went through what he did. I think right about now he needs to know you still think he's worthy of your love."

Eve got to her feet, and Burl curved his arm around her shoulder. Tears blurred her eyes as she looked up at her father's face. "I don't know, Daddy. I think it's too late for that. I don't imagine Elliot wants to see me."

"It's worth giving it a try, isn't it?"

Eve gave him a smile, then reached over and hugged his massive chest. "You're right, Daddy. I'll go see him tomorrow. And thanks for making me feel a little better."

Burl patted his daughter's cheek with affection. "That's what daddies are for, darlin'. Now let's go eat some of Marcia's ribs before she gets mad at both of us."

Five miles away, Elliot lay on the dock staring up at the stars. Rebel's nose rested across his midsection. Elliot absently stroked the hound's head and ears as his mind kept up a tormented journey through the past week.

Elliot could not put Eve out of his thoughts. Not even for a minute. And he was beginning to wonder about his sanity. He couldn't eat or sleep, he couldn't think, he couldn't quit hurting. Even out of sight she had a grip on him as tight as any vise.

He had often heard that love was more powerful than anything. He'd scoffed at that notion. But now, after falling in love with Eve, he was beginning to agree.

"She thinks I still want to be a cop, Rebel," he told the hound.

At the sound of his name, the dog lifted his head, looked at Elliot and let out a soulful whine. Elliot rubbed Rebel's loose skin. "I know boy. It struck me the same way," Elliot said grimly.

He could still hear her soft voice telling him that a policeman was what he was, and that nothing or no one should take that away from him. He knew she was right. Deep down he knew that everything she'd said to him had made sense. At the time he just hadn't wanted to admit it. He'd been angry with her because she wouldn't let him settle for less.

Eve had said he wasn't a fighter, but actually he'd been fighting for a long time. Since the night he'd left Fort Worth, he supposed. He'd been fighting a battle with himself. Eve had just forced him to realize that. She'd made him see he couldn't live happily with a war waging silently inside him. He did want to be a cop.

But, oh God, was he ready to go back? he wondered. Was he ready to open himself up to all of that again?

Maybe, maybe not, he thought. But he did know one thing. He loved Eve. He wanted them to be together and happy. And that wasn't going to happen unless he took control of things and made it happen.

Before Rebel could figure out what had happened to his pillow, Elliot was off the dock and headed on the path back to the house.

Once there, he went straight to his bedroom and pulled two suitcases from the closet. Determinedly he went about packing his clothes, thinking as he did that it was the first positive thing he'd done in a long time.

Eve woke up the next morning to the shrill sound of the telephone in her ear. The caller was Marcia, and from the sound of her voice she was frantic.

"Get Burl over here to the restaurant," she said. "Pronto. The beef freezer has gone on the blink. Everything is thawing!"

Eve rubbed a hand across her sleepy face. "I'll send him right over."

After her father had left the house to check out the problem at the restaurant, Eve threw off her robe and began to dress.

She was going to see Elliot today, she thought while brushing her long hair. Judging from the last time she'd seen him, he'd probably give her a cool reception, but she wasn't going to let that put her off. She loved him; she had to make him see that they belonged together.

Daybreak still hadn't arrived when Eve walked over to the restaurant. She would help Marcia find a place to pack the extra meat away before she cooked breakfast for herself and Burl. Then she would drive over to Elliot's.

Eve found the kitchen in utter chaos, with Marcia down on her knees, throwing wrapped packages of beef into a cardboard box. Burl and Bob were tilting the broken freezer onto a loading dolly.

"Can I help?" she asked

"Get your pickup and bring it right up to the back door," her father said.

Eve hurried back outside and climbed into her old Ford. She had the truck backed up and the tailgate down by the time the two men had maneuvered the freezer through the kitchen.

"Evie," Burl said, once the two men had loaded the empty freezer. "I want you to drive this thing over to San Augustine to the repair shop."

Eve's mouth dropped open with disappointment. Didn't her father remember she was going to see Elliot? "Me? But I—"

Burl sighed. "I know you were going to drive over to see Elliot. But I'm going to be busy. You won't have to stay until it's ready," he added. "Tell Leo I'll pay him plenty extra to deliver it back to us."

Eve tried not to show her frustration. "But what about Bob? He could take it."

Burl shook his head. "He's laying tile in the bathroom of Cabin 8. It has to be ready by tomorrow."

Eve could understand that. She'd already reserved the room for tomorrow night. She nodded. "Okay, I'll leave right after breakfast."

An hour after Eve had left with the freezer, Elliot parked his Jeep in front of the Pine Ridge restaurant. He hadn't found Eve at the house or the motel office, so he figured she was probably helping with the breakfast crowd.

Faye was waiting on tables. He stood by the cashier's counter until he could catch her attention.

The tall woman finished refilling a man's coffee cup, then walked over to Elliot.

"Well, hello, Elliot," she said with a wide smile. "You hunting Eve?"

He nodded. "Is she back in the kitchen?"

Faye shook her head. "No. She's gone over to San Augustine."

Elliot had to hold his tongue to keep from cursing out his frustration. "When will she be back?"

Faye shrugged. "I don't really know. Mr. Crawford could probably tell you, but he's taken a boat over to another marina to have it repaired."

Elliot said nothing as he tried to decide what to do. He had to return the dog to his rightful owner. He didn't want to leave without seeing Eve, but Rebel and his bags were already loaded in the Jeep. Caleb was going to meet him in less than thirty minutes to pick up the dog. If he missed him, he'd have to drive a hundred fifty miles out of the way to get the dog back to his permanent home.

"Why don't you just sit down and have some breakfast," Faye suggested. "Surely Eve will be back in a little while. Unless she decided to go shopping or something."

Elliot shook his head. "I can't stay that long. I have to meet someone. Just tell her I came by to see her and—" He stopped. What else could he say? He wanted to tell Eve that he loved her, that he'd decided he was a fighter after all and that when he was certain of things he'd be back for her. But he couldn't relay such a message through this woman.

He merely shook his head and started toward the door. "Just tell her I came by to see her," he said again. "And that I'll be back."

"When?" Faye asked, knowing Eve would want to know.

Elliot shrugged. There was no way he could answer that. "I don't know, Faye. Just tell her sometime. Sometime soon."

Eve didn't bother to stop at Pine Ridge when she returned from San Augustine. Instead, she headed straight to the turnoff for Elliot's house.

The five miles of dirt road seemed endless. While Eve steered the pickup around the roughest patches in the road, she thought about all the things she wanted to say to Elliot. She wanted him to know that she wasn't trying to pressure him. She didn't know exactly how to tell him that, but she did know how to tell him she loved him. That would be a start. If only he would give her the chance.

Eve knew something was different the moment she stopped the Ford in front of the gate. The door was shut, and all the windows closed. Since there was no air-conditioning in the house, Elliot never shut the windows, even when he was gone.

She climbed out slowly while keeping her eyes on the front door.

"Elliot?" Eve called as she climbed the steps.

Everything was silent. She whistled for Rebel, but the dog didn't appear. A choking panic rose up in Eve as she hurried around to the back of the house.

There was nothing on the back porch. The lawn chairs and the little wooden table where she and Elliot had eaten on the night he'd proposed to her were nowhere in sight, nor was Rebel's food bowl.

She walked across the porch and tried the back door. It was locked. Eve cupped her hands around her eyes and peered through the glass. The kitchen looked bare. It was enough proof for Eve to know that he was gone.

Tears scalded her eyes. For a moment she allowed the sobs that were choking her throat to be released.

He was well and truly gone from her life now. And she hated herself for not coming to see him sooner. If she had, things might be different now. Elliot might still be here.

Eve wearily made her way off the front porch, then sat down on the back steps. Her shoulders slumped as tears continued to roll down her cheeks. She had never been a whiner or a crier. Burl had raised her to be a battler, and she'd always faced things with single-minded determination. But losing Elliot this way seemed to crumble all her strength.

An hour passed before Eve forced herself to walk to her truck. On the drive home she asked herself over and over how Elliot could just go without saying something to her. Had she meant so little to him? Had it been that easy to forget her?

Feeling she couldn't face anyone just yet, Eve went straight to the bungalow. She spent long minutes in the bathroom sluicing her face with cold water in an effort to wash away the ravages of her tears.

Elliot's leaving shouldn't have hurt and shocked her so. He'd already ended their relationship. But it did hurt. Deep down Eve had still hoped they could work things out. Obviously she'd been all wrong about that.

Eve was in the kitchen filling a glass with iced tea when the telephone rang. Sniffing, she lifted the receiver and hoped her voice sounded normal.

"Hello."

"Eve, are you busy?"

It was Faye calling from the restaurant. Eve hoped

they didn't need her help. It would be impossible for her to put on a cheery face and wait tables today.

"No, I'm just having a glass of tea."

"Well, I just thought you might like to know that that man of yours was here this morning."

Eve gripped the receiver. "You—you mean Elliot."

"Why sure I mean Elliot," she drawled. "Who'd you think I meant?"

Eve couldn't believe it. Elliot was here this morning? "What was he doing? What did he say?" She fired the questions at Faye.

"Said he was looking for you. I told him you were gone, you'd be back later. I told him to have breakfast and wait but he said he didn't have time, that he had to meet someone."

"Who?" Eve swiftly asked.

"Now, Eve, do I look like a woman who pokes her nose into into other people's business?" Faye asked in feigned innocence.

"Yes, you do!"

Faye chuckled. "Well, I didn't this time, girl. He just said to tell you he came by to see you. And that he'd be back sometime. That's all I know."

Eve wiped a shaky hand across her forehead. "Okay, Faye. Thanks for letting me know."

After hanging up the receiver Eve paced the kitchen floor. Elliot had been to see her. But he'd left to go meet someone. Faye's information played over and over in her mind. Where would he be going? she asked herself. And who did he know around here besides Caleb?

Caleb! Eve ran to the living room and began to thumb through a telephone book. Once she'd found the number, she hurriedly placed the call.

The woman answering informed her that Caleb was out, but that she would leave him a message to call Eve.

Eve had to settle for that. But she was desperate by the time two hours had passed and the telephone finally rang.

"Miss Eve? This is Caleb Jones here," the voice said.

Eve felt weak with relief. "Thank you for calling, Mr. Jones. I know you're a busy man."

"I'm never too busy to oblige a pretty lady."

Any other time, Eve would have smiled at his compliment, but it just wasn't in her today. "I—I was wondering if you'd seen Elliot?"

The line was silent for a moment. Eve's heart began to race with worry. She was almost ready to shout a question at him when he said, "I saw Elliot this morning. Didn't you?"

Eve tried to swallow down the thickness in her throat. "No. I'm afraid I was out when Elliot came by. I—I went over to his house. Everything was shut up—" It was so awful knowing that this man knew more about Elliot than she did herself.

"Well, I figured you knew, Miss Eve," Caleb drawled. "Elliot's gone back to Fort Worth."

Eve stared at the floor in stunned silence. Gone back to Fort Worth? But that was the thing he kept insisting he wouldn't do!

No, she silently corrected herself. He wouldn't go back to the police department. He probably didn't have anything against the city itself. After all, it was his home, she thought dismally.

"But what—what does that mean, Mr. Jones? Is he going back to the police department?"

"Hmm, well, Miss Eve, I just couldn't say about that. You know Elliot. He can be real closed-mouthed about things. I tried to get it out of him, but he wouldn't say much. But I'd be willing to bet you'll be hearing from him in a few days."

Eve doubted that, but she wasn't going to go into it with this man. Elliot has told Faye he'd be back sometime, but sometime was a very evasive word, promising nothing.

"Thank you again for taking the time to call," she told him.

"It was no trouble at all," he assured her. "And if I hear from Elliot, I'll let you know."

Eve thanked him once again, then slowly hung up the receiver. She felt numb, and she wasn't sure if she wanted to cry or scream.

That Elliot had gone back to Fort Worth was the last thing she'd expected to hear, and her mind began to race frantically in search of answers. But there just weren't any answers for Eve.

She could only guess his intentions. And the only thing she could come up with was that he'd gone back to turn in his resignation. Maybe he'd come by to tell Eve that. Or maybe he'd come by to tell her a final goodbye. Either thought was unbearable to her.

The next week was very difficult for Eve. She tried to stay as busy as possible and keep a smile on her face in front of everyone, but Elliot's departure had levied a heavy toll on her heart.

She was so dispirited that nothing mattered to her. She didn't feel a spark of excitement about starting college or about anything else that had been important to her before she'd met Elliot.

By the end of the second week, Eve had sunk into a resigned depression. Elliot was not coming back. She had to face the realization. Eve just didn't know how she was going to do that.

Late one evening, three weeks after Elliot had left, Eve was down on her hands and knees weeding her flower garden when her father's shadow crossed her work area.

Shading her eyes, Eve looked up at him.

"Hello, Daddy. Need something?"

He'd been working on income tax papers, and she expected him to say he couldn't find a bill or receipt.

Burl shook his head. "I thought we might take a little spin out on the lake."

Eve smiled and brushed her grubby hands against her jeans. The past few days her father had gone out of his way to spend extra time with her. Burl seemed to know how devastated she'd been over losing Elliot. Eve loved her father for knowing and caring. She'd never known her mother, but Burl had always tried his best to fill that void in Eve's life.

"I'd like that," she told him.

Minutes later, Burl and Eve walked out on the dock and climbed into the red fishing boat that Eve had been driving the night she'd first met Elliot.

Eve always loved being out on the water, and this evening was no exception. The hot, muggy air had cooled somewhat with the falling of the sun, and the rush of the wind against her face and hair was refreshing.

The two of them had traveled about ten minutes when Burl slackened the speed and reached for his rod and reel. Eve smiled knowingly at her father as they drifted to a stop near a grassy point.

"I thought this was going to be a boat ride," she said teasingly.

"It was," Burl said with a chuckle. "But I heard the big one calling out there."

"You don't take off time enough for yourself, Daddy," she told him. "I'll bet you haven't fished in over a month."

"Well, darlin', it takes a lot of work to keep the marina going."

A sad look crossed Eve's face. Her father saw it and frowned.

"What's the matter?"

Eve sighed and combed her windblown hair back from her face with her fingers. "Nothing. I'm just wondering how people let their priorities get so mixed up."

"Meaning?" Burl asked as he cast the fishing line out across the water.

Eve shrugged, unaware that there was a defeated sag to her shoulders.

"These past three weeks I've been asking myself what is really the most important thing in my life."

Burl began to slowly crank in the fishing line. "And what did you decide that was?"

"Elliot," she said quietly,

Burl turned his head to look at her. "I know his leaving has hurt you, Evie. I hate that it ended like this for you."

Eve shook her head and looked out over the lake. Tears glistened in her eyes, and she stifled the sobs in her throat. "I messed up everything, Daddy," she said miserably. "I kept harping at Elliot about his career, how he shouldn't throw it away, how he should fight for decency and honor." She stopped long enough to swallow and wipe her eyes. "I should have just accepted him the way he wanted—"

Burl reached over and patted her shoulder. "You're

being too hard on yourself, Eve. I expect you and Elliot just met at the wrong time."

She heaved out a heavy sigh. "Well, I guess none of that matters anymore. He's gone. I'll probably never hear from him again."

Toledo Bend was a fickle lake. It could be a calm lamb one minute and a roaring tiger the next.

Just before Burl and Eve decided to return to the marina, thunderheads began to roll in along with a brisk south wind.

The lake was white-capped by the time they reached the halfway point home. The red fishing boat rolled and pitched with the bucking waves. Burl skillfully managed to ride out each swell without getting the boat swamped.

Eve wasn't frightened by the rough water. Her father was very good with a boat. She knew he could get them home safely. It would only take them much longer than under normal conditions.

It started to rain just before they pulled beneath the covered boat dock back at Pine Ridge. Eve didn't bother reaching for a slicker. She and Burl were already sopping wet from the spray of the waves. It would be pointless to worry about the rain.

Burl shut off the motor and jumped out to moor the boat. Eve followed at a slower pace, wringing the water from her hair as she went.

"I was worried about you two."

The deep voice sounded behind her, making her jerk around in sudden fright. She was even more shocked to see Elliot standing at the far end of the dock.

"Elliot!" Eve was unaware she whispered his name.

She was so stunned to see him that she stood rooted to the dock, staring at him through her wet, tangled hair.

Burl was the first one to make a move. He walked down the planked walkway and reached out for Elliot's hand.

"Glad to see you again, son. Looks like you got here just in time for a thunderstorm."

Elliot smiled and shook Burl's hand. It meant a lot to him to be greeted warmly by Eve's father. "I'm glad. Fort Worth was as hot as a firecracker when I left."

Burl gave him a hefty pat on the upper arm and motioned his head back in Eve's direction as if to say, Handle her carefully. "I'll see you two up at the house," he told Elliot, then left in the direction of the bungalow.

Even though the weather was very warm, Eve began to shiver as Elliot walked toward her.

His hair had been cut to a shorter length, but other than that he still looked like her dear, familiar Elliot.

She forced her legs to move forward.

"Elliot," she repeated once again.

He began to walk rapidly toward her. Then suddenly he stopped, his eyes focused on her face, and Eve could see the uncertainty in them. "Are you glad to see me, Eve?"

The question seemed insane to Eve. Didn't he know that was the only thing in the world she'd wanted, to see him again?

She ran to him, a sob slipping past her lips as she flung her arms around his waist.

Elliot gathered her tightly against him, closing his eyes as he relished the feel of her soft body against him.

"I thought I'd never see you again, Elliot," she

murmured. "Why did you just go like that? Why haven't you called? I thought—"

"After we argued, I was miserable as hell. I had to do something. Oh, Eve, I've missed you so," he groaned, pressing his cheek against her wet hair. "These past weeks have been torment without you. But I knew you wanted me to be sure about things. And I wanted to be sure about things before I talked to you again."

She suddenly pushed away from his chest and looked up at him through misty gray eyes. "So why are you here, Elliot?"

He laughed. Her question was just like the straightforward Eve he'd first met in the fog.

"I'm here to tell you that I love you. That I still want you to marry me."

"I didn't think you—oh, Elliot, I'm so sorry I was stubborn and pushy and—"

He gave her shoulders a little shake, smiling as he did. "And I'm sorry I didn't listen to you a lot sooner. You were right. I couldn't offer you any kind of life when a part of mine was still tied up with the past."

Eve brought her hands around to his face, cradling the masculine beauty between her palms. "What happened Elliot, when you went back? Did you go to the—"

"Department?" he finished for her. He nodded. "And you know what? It felt good, Eve. It felt damn good."

Eve felt weak with relief and happiness. "Oh, Elliot, I'm—I'm so glad," she said, then began to cry softly against his shoulder.

Elliot stroked her hair, her back, the sweet curve of her cheek. "I know now that I can't make things the way they were before the cattle scandal happened. But I've come to realize that I don't want them to be that way. Back then I was too caught up in my work to know that my life was lacking in other ways. I'd buried myself so deeply I was blind to what Yates and Delvecchio were doing."

She looked up at him. "Are the two men still there?"

He chuckled smugly. "You should have seen their faces when I walked into the precinct."

"They'll try to get you again," Eve said with certainty.

"That's what I'm counting on, Eve. I'll be ready, and they'll get their due. In the meantime, do you think you're ready to be this cop's wife?"

"Only if I know one thing," she told him.

"What's that?" he asked

"That you went back because you really wanted to. That you're going to go on with your career as a policeman because it's what you really want."

He didn't say anything, and Eve held his gaze as he pulled her up on tiptoes and covered her mouth with his.

For long moments he let his kiss tell her what he wanted to say and what she needed to hear. Eve clung to him as she kissed him back with all the hunger she'd felt these past weeks.

After a while Elliot spoke. "I always wanted to be a cop, Eve. I'd just let bitterness color everything in my life—until you came along. You made me see that love is stronger than hate or revenge. You made me see that fighting for what's good and decent is as much a part of me as you are. Injustices in the law are always going to happen. I've come to realize that. But that's just one of the hazards of the job. And maybe somewhere along the way I'll make a difference in someone else's life."

"I love you, Elliot," she said simply and sweetly.

"And no matter what kind of injustices we have to face, we'll face them together. Always together."

He kissed her again. After he drew back, Eve let her eyes roam his precious features; her finger touched the scar on his lip. "You know, Joe Elliot, you've never told me how you got this scar."

He suddenly laughed, and Eve knew it was a laugh filled with true happiness. She knew as she looked into his eyes that all the haunted shadows of the past were gone.

"How do you think I got it, nosy?" he teased. "With a beer bottle in some sleazy bar? A fistfight in a back alley?"

She smiled. "Something like that."

He reached up and thoughtfully touched his lip. "This was from a fastball pitched by a thirteen-year-old boy. His daddy was a partner of mine, and we were trying to give the boy some pitching tips. Unfortunately, his arm control hadn't quite developed."

"Dirty business," Eve said with a laugh. "I expect you don't tell that too often, in fear of ruining your tough image."

"It's one of the skeletons in my closet," he teased, then turned her around and began to guide her off the dock. "You need to get out of those wet clothes. And I'm sure Burl is wondering what's going on."

Eve curled her arm around the back of his waist as they walked along through the rain. "Daddy's given me a very bad time over you," she confessed to Elliot. "He says I badgered you and that I went at you like a bull with horns."

Elliot let out a howl of laughter. "I can already see he's going to be a great daddy-in-law."

"Humph." Eve tried to sound offended, but a giggle got in the way.

He hugged her shoulder as they continued to walk

toward the bungalow. "I can't wait to get you to Fort Worth, Eve," he told her. "We're going to make a great pair, you know. You a lawyer and me a cop." He winked down at her. "Just think of all the inside information I can give you."

Eve grinned beguilingly up at him. "Is it permissible for cops and lawyers to sleep together?"

He gave her a serious sidelong glance. "If they have a license."

Eve laughed and Elliot grinned.

"I've found a college for you. It's not far from where we'll be living. And they have a strong law program there."

She was deeply touched to know that he'd already been thinking of her wants, too. "It sounds wonderful."

"Eve—there's something else I haven't gotten around to asking you."

"What's that?" Eve asked dreamily

"Well, I've been thinking we might want a child. Do you think we could work a baby in there somewhere along the way?"

Inside, Eve was shouting with joy, but on the outside she gave him a stern look.

"If we have a license."

This time Elliot laughed and Eve grinned.

"My captain is anxious to meet you."

"You told him about me?" she asked, both pleased and surprised.

"Of course."

"Are you going to drive me around downtown on your Harley?" she asked, then went on before he had the opportunity to answer. "I'm going to get me a pair of tight leather pants, and then you can use me as a decoy on one of your vice stakeouts."

Elliot laughed heartily and reached over and gave Eve's chin an affectionate shake. "Eve, darlin', you've watched too much TV," he drawled.

From inside the bungalow, Burl watched Eve and Elliot cross the lawn. A smile passed over the older man's face as he watched the love flow back and forth between them.

Thirty years ago it had been the same for him and Eve's mother. And that was why he knew Eve and Elliot belonged together. Why they would always be happy with each other.

Turning away from the window, Burl went to the door to let his family in.

Epilogue

The spring night was warm as a car cruised out of downtown Fort Worth and headed toward a suburban country home.

Inside the car, Eve allowed her head to fall back against the seat. "My feet are aching, and I'm exhausted," Eve said, then looked over at her husband and gave him a warm contented smile. "But I've never been happier," she added.

"It was very nice of Burl to drive all that way to be here tonight. I wish he would have stayed over. But I know this is a busy time for him at the marina."

"I was glad Daddy could make it," she agreed, then added, "It was thoughtful of Caleb to be here tonight, too. By the way, you looked very handsome when you went up on stage."

He gave her a cocky grin as he steered the car

through the thinning traffic. "So you like your husband being in the spotlight."

"As far as I'm concerned, my husband is always in the spotlight. But it's even nicer when everyone else knows about it."

Tonight an awards banquet had been held for the Fort Worth Police Department. Eve had sat out in the audience and proudly watched as her husband was presented a special plaque for outstanding service in the line of duty. It had been one of the happiest moments of Eve's life.

"I think you might be a little bit prejudiced, darlin'," Elliot drawled.

Eve scooted across the seat and snuggled her cheek against his shoulder. "Of course I am," she murmured happily. "You're my husband, the daddy of my baby girl, and you're also the best cop this ole town ever had."

"Flatterer," he said with a deep laugh.

A few minutes later the two of them arrived home. It was a simple country house with a wide porch overlooking a small lawn. Elliot and Eve enjoyed it because they were away from the hustle and bustle of the city, but were still close enough to commute to work and school.

Elliot paid the babysitter, then went straight to the nursery to check on his eight-month-old daughter, Megan.

Eve stayed behind in the living room, wanting to give her husband the pleasure of a moment alone with his child. Elliot loved their daughter very much and spent as much time with her as he possibly could on his off hours.

Even though she and Elliot led busy lives, having the baby had rounded out their love. Elliot's lack of family in the past made him all the more appreciative of Eve and Megan.

Kicking off her high heels, she began to pull the hairpins from the coil at the back of her head. Once the dark tresses were lying free around her shoulders, she picked up the plaque from where Elliot had tossed it onto the couch.

She was trying to decide in which part of the room to display it when Elliot slipped up behind her and latched his arms around her waist.

"Is Megan all right?" she asked, loving the feel of him as he pulled her back against his long, hard body.

"Sleeping peacefully," he said, nuzzling his cheek against her soft hair.

"I'll check in on her in a minute," Eve told him. "I was just trying to decide where your plaque would look best. Or would you rather take it back to your office?"

He turned her around in his arms. Eve looked up at him and smiled, noticing he'd taken off his suit jacket and tie. She slid her hands up the sleeves of his white shirt, then linked them over his shoulders.

"No, I don't want to take it to the office," he told her. "I'm giving it to you. It's really yours, anyway."

"Elliot, be serious."

"I couldn't be more serious," he said, then leaned down and placed a lingering kiss on her lips. "I wouldn't even be a policeman tonight if it hadn't been for you. Much less have been credited for outstanding service."

"Elliot, you're giving me too much credit. You're the one who's done all the hard work. All I've done is be here to encourage you."

His hands came up to frame her face. "You make it all mean more, Eve. Without you, that plaque wouldn't mean half as much."

"It's been over five years since I drifted up to you and

Rebel in those woods. That night I didn't realize just how unhappy and torn you were. But it didn't take me long to figure out that you still wanted to be a cop."

Elliot chuckled, and then his eyes filled with tenderness as he remembered how she'd looked across the camp fire, and how badly he'd wanted to make love to her. She had filled him with fresh feelings and new hope. From the time he'd realized he loved her, his life had taken on a whole different meaning.

"We've come a long way since then, Eve. You've finished college and started on your law degree, along with giving me a beautiful daughter," he added with an immeasurable amount of pride.

"And you've made an endless number of major arrests. Including Yates and Delvecchio. The whole city was stirred up over that one."

He shook his head as he thought of the two officers who'd once been good cops, but somewhere along the way greed had overridden their decency and honor. It had taken Elliot over a year to gather enough evidence to arrest and convict the two men. But the time had not mattered to Elliot. As he had told Eve, he hadn't been out for revenge for what they'd done to him, he'd merely been a cop doing his job.

"When I left Fort Worth and went back to east Texas I thought those two guys had won. I thought I'd lost everything because of them—my self-worth, my beliefs, the respect of my coworkers, my friends. But you were right, Eve, when you said that sometimes when you're knocked down you come out of things even better. And things couldn't be any better for me now."

Eve gave him a lazy, provocative smile and began

undoing the buttons on his shirt. "Surely I could make things a little bit better. I'd love to try, anyway."

A sexy glint filled his eyes as his fingers slid across her shoulder and up her bare neck.

"You think so, do you?" he asked cockily as he unhooked an earring from her earlobe.

"Yes. I think so," she answered with feminine certainty.

Pushing aside the tails of his shirt, Eve slid her hands up his chest. A husky laugh gurgled in Elliot's throat, and he reached over and switched off the table lamp.

Eve stood waiting in the darkness for his hands to return to her. When they did, his fingers found the zipper at the center of her back. Her heart beat with eager anticipation as he pulled it downward until the blue evening dress was lying in a soft heap at her feet.

Elliot lifted her in his arms, then kissed her with such promise that it curled Eve's toes.

"Tonight we're going to celebrate," he murmured.

"Mmm. Sounds wonderful," she whispered, clinging tightly to his neck. "What are we celebrating? You getting the award?"

He began to carry her in the direction of their bedroom. "Being recognized as a good policeman is nice. But not nearly as nice as having you, Eve. So tonight we're celebrating our love."

Eve's heart swelled as she thought of how much she loved this man. Snuggling her cheek against his, she echoed his words.

"Our love."

* * * * *

Fall in Love with...

MEN
in UNIFORM

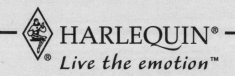

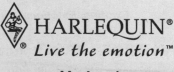

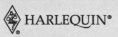

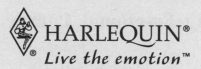

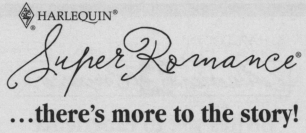
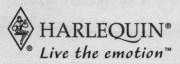

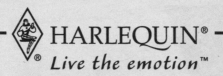